# No More
## Dead Dogs

# No More
## Dead Dogs

## gordon korman

Disney • HYPERION

Los Angeles   New York

First Hardcover Edition, September 2000
First Paperback Edition, October 2002
New Paperback Edition, June 2017

10 9 8 7 6 5 4
FAC-025438-19270
Printed in the United States of America

This book is set in 12-point Janson Text Lt Pro/Fontspring

Library of Congress Control Number for Hardcover Edition: 00024313
ISBN 978-1-4847-9844-7
Visit www.DisneyBooks.com

SUSTAINABLE
FORESTRY
INITIATIVE
Certified Chain of Custody
Promoting Sustainable Forestry
www.sfiprogram.org
SFI-01054
The SFI label applies to the text stock

*For M. Jerry Weiss,*
*who has been encouraging me to write about*
*Rick-isms since the eternal equinox*

# Cast of characters

### The football players:
Hero . . . . . . . . . . . . . . . Wallace Wallace
Quarterback . . . . . . . . . . . Rick Falconi
Celery Eater . . . . . . . . . . . Feather Wrigley
Ex–Best Friend . . . . . . . . . . Steve Cavanaugh

### The drama club:
Actress. . . . . . . . . . . . . . Rachel Turner
Co-star . . . . . . . . . . . . . . Trudi Davis
Insect . . . . . . . . . . . . . . Nathaniel Spitzner
Cast and Crew . . . . . . . . . . Vito Brundia
Leticia Ogden
Leo Samuels
Everton Wu
Kelly Ramone

### The adults:
Director . . . . . . . . . . . . . Mr. Fogelman
Coach . . . . . . . . . . . . . . Coach Wrigley
Mom . . . . . . . . . . . . . . . Mrs. Wallace

### And featuring:
Porker Zit . . . . . . . . . . . . Parker Schmidt
Rollerblader . . . . . . . . . . . Rory Piper
Kid Brother. . . . . . . . . . . . Dylan Turner
Road Rage . . . . . . . . . . . . Laszlo Tamas

And special guests the *Dead Mangoes*

Old Shep appears courtesy of Zack Paris Enterprises, XK-9

The characters in this book are fictional. Any resemblance you may find to actual persons or dogs, living or dead, proves that you have a lot of strange friends.

# Enter...

# WALLACE WALLACE

**W**HEN MY DAD was a helicopter pilot in Vietnam, he once rescued eight Navy SEALs who were stranded behind enemy lines. He flew back using only his left hand, because the right one had taken a bullet. With the chopper on fire, and running on an empty tank and just gas fumes, he managed to outmaneuver a squadron of MiG fighters and make it safely home to base.

That was my favorite story when I was small. It was also a total pack of lies. The bullet "scar" on Dad's arm was really left over from a big infected pimple. And by the time I was old enough to do the math,

I realized that when the war ended in Vietnam, my father was fourteen.

I was pretty clueless, like little kids can be. I thought my parents had a great relationship. The only thing they ever fought about was lying. And even then the arguments were short: Mom wanted the truth, and Dad wouldn't recognize it if it danced up and bit him on the nose.

But even though I didn't really understand what was going on, I guess it percolated down to me somehow. The more Dad lied, the more I told the truth.

My earliest memory is of my mother complaining that the laundry had shrunk her new pants.

"Your pants didn't get smaller, Mommy," I assured her. "Your butt got bigger."

Little kids get away with that kind of stuff, so she laughed it off.

But she wasn't laughing three years later when the next-door neighbor asked my opinion of her light and fluffy cake.

I thought it over. "It tastes like vacuum cleaner fuzz. And the icing reminds me of antifreeze."

"Wally, how could you *say* such a thing?" my mother wailed when we got home.

"Mom," I asked, "did Dad really miss my birthday party because he had to visit a sick friend?"

It didn't matter that she didn't answer. I had already seen the hotel bill on my father's night table. The Desert Inn, Las Vegas.

I was more stuck on the truth than ever. For me, honesty wasn't just the best policy; it was the only one.

I told my soon-to-be ex-piano teacher that her fingernails reminded me of velociraptor claws. The cook at summer camp I informed that his pork chop could double as a bulletproof vest. My cousin Melinda's clarinet playing I described as "somebody strangling a duck."

"Must you be so—you know—colorful?" my mother moaned.

"When it's the truth," I said firmly.

"But the Abernathys are so proud of their new house! Did you have to announce that it's built on a slant?"

"It *is*! I dropped my yo-yo, and it rolled all the way to the kitchen."

"Wally," she pleaded, "how can I make you understand—"

I used to wonder if things would have been different

if I'd had the guts to tell my dad that he didn't have to be a war hero or an astronaut or a CIA agent. It was enough for me that he was my dad.

I almost did it once. I was so close! But before I could get my mouth open, he said, "Wally, have I ever told you about the time I led a crew that put out oil well fires?"

Oil well fires.

So I gave up, and, eventually, so did Mom. I was in fifth grade when they got their divorce. By then, I wouldn't have told a lie at gunpoint.

That's why I never once complained about the black eye I got for telling Buzz Bolitsky he had the IQ of a Ring Ding. You won't see me crying over the fact that I haven't received a birthday present from Uncle Ted for two years. The fact is, Uncle Ted's toupee really *did* look like a small animal had crawled up onto his head and died there. If he didn't want the truth, he shouldn't have said those fateful words: "Do you notice anything different about me?"

So when Mr. Fogelman had us write book reviews in eighth-grade English, I wasn't trying to be rude or disrespectful or even smart-alecky. I gave Fogelman what I give everybody—the truth, the whole truth, and nothing but the truth:

*Old Shep, My Pal* by Zack Paris is the most boring book I've read in my entire life. I did not have a favorite character. I hated everybody equally. The most interesting part came on the last page where it said "The End." This book couldn't be any lousier if it came with a letter bomb. I would not recommend it to my worst enemy.

Mr. Fogelman scanned the few lines, and glared at me, face flaming in anger. "This isn't what I assigned!"

I should say that I had nothing against Mr. Fogelman at that moment. He was okay—the kind of young teacher who tries to be "one of the guys," but everything he does only shows how out of it he is. I just wanted to set the record straight.

"Yes, it is," I told him. "The assignment sheet said to give our honest opinion, write what was our favorite part and character, and make a recommendation. It's all there."

"*Old Shep, My Pal* is a timeless classic!" roared the teacher. "It won the Gunhold Award! It was my favorite book growing up. Everybody loves it." He turned to the rest of the class. "Right?"

The reaction was a murmur of mixed reviews.

"It was okay, I guess."

"Not too bad."

"Why did it have to be so sad?"

"Exactly!" Fogelman pounced on the comment. "It *was* sad. What a heartbreaking surprise ending!"

"I wasn't surprised," I said. "I knew Old Shep was going to die before I started page one."

"Don't be ridiculous," the teacher snapped. "How?"

I shrugged. "Because the dog always dies. Go to the library and pick out a book with an award sticker and a dog on the cover. Trust me, that dog is going down."

"Not true!" stormed Mr. Fogelman.

"Well," I challenged, "what happened to Old Yeller?"

"Oh, all right," the teacher admitted. "So Old Yeller died."

"What about Sounder?" piped up Joey Quick.

"And Bristle Face," added Mike "Feather" Wrigley, one of my football teammates.

"Don't forget *Where the Red Fern Grows*," I put in. "The double whammy—*two* dogs die in that one."

"You've made your point," growled Mr. Fogelman. "And now I'm going to make mine. I expect a proper review. And you're going to give it to me—during detention!"

6

"Nice grab, Wallace!"

I caught the short pass, and turned upfield.

*WHAM!*

Steve Cavanaugh hit me at hip level, and I saw stars. It was a clean tackle—totally legal—but it was pretty hard for practice. This had less to do with Cavanaugh's toughness than it did with the fact that we used to be best friends.

"Steve, are you crazy?"

Cavanaugh's body was yanked off of me, and the face of Rick Falconi, our quarterback, took its place in my field of vision.

"Wallace, are you okay? Speak to me!"

I pushed him away and jumped up. "I'm fine, Rick. It was a legal hit."

Rick looked daggers at Cavanaugh. "You *idiot*! You could've injured our best player. Why'd you have to nail him?"

Cavanaugh pulled off his helmet, and down cascaded the longest, blondest hair at Bedford Middle School. "What did you want me to do? Give him a pedicure?"

If there was one thing Cavanaugh had more of than hair, it was sarcasm.

"I'm not the best player," I told Rick.

"Yes, you are," Rick countered.

"I scored one touchdown all year," I insisted.

"Well, Jackass Jackass," my ex–best friend reminded me, "one is a pretty big number for a guy who spent the whole season on the bench."

"One is all it takes," Rick pointed out, "when it comes with three seconds to go in the county championship."

Okay, that part was true. Actually, I was only on the field as a blocker. But Rick panicked, and handed off too high, stuffing the ball into my ex–best friend's face, jamming it between the mouth guard and the visor. Poor Cavanaugh never saw the two linebackers who sandwiched him. The ball popped out. It sailed over the heads of both teams, and blooped into the end zone.

"It was a total fluke," I insisted. "Anybody could've jumped on that ball."

"But *you* did," Rick told me. "And we won the championship."

They just didn't get it. It would have been great to be a football titan if it was the *truth*. But to act like an all-star when I was really a pretty mediocre player—that was almost as bad as lying.

I didn't give in. "Why does that make *me* the hero? Why not Cavanaugh's face, or even you, Rick? Without that bonehead handoff, we probably would have lost."

"Hey, man," Rick said angrily. "Deep, deep down, a tiny little part of my brain sensed that I needed to do that. It was, you know, subhuman."

"You mean subconscious," I supplied.

"Whatever."

At that moment, Feather sprinted up, with two of the defensive backs hot on his heels. "What's going on?" he panted. "Did Wallace get hurt?"

"He's fine," Cavanaugh assured him. My ex–best friend sounded disappointed.

In a way, I couldn't blame him. I was getting all this credit for being the best player, which is what Cavanaugh really *was*. He was an explosive receiver with great hands, he ran like a deer, and he could cover any position on defense. He was even the kicker, so good field position, extra points, and field goals all came from him. He ate right and worked out like a maniac. As team captain he had every reason to expect to be admired.

I didn't blame him for hating me; I blamed him for being a total jerk about everything else.

"Uh-oh," Feather said suddenly. "Quit goofing off. Here comes my dad."

His father, Coach Wrigley, jogged up, blowing sharp blasts on his whistle. "Wait a minute, Wallace! What are you doing here?"

The coach always called us by our last names, which in my case, made no difference. "Short passes, Coach."

"Not today," said Wrigley. "You're supposed to be on detention right now."

I gazed over the coach's shoulder. There, at the edge of the field, stood Mr. Fogelman.

*"Detention?"* repeated Rick. "But our first game is tomorrow."

"He should have thought of that before opening up his big mouth to Mr. Fogelman," growled Coach Wrigley.

"I'm ready for tomorrow," I assured Rick.

My ex–best friend reached out and patted the seat of my pants with his helmet. "I agree. Your butt is in perfect shape. Get ready to sit on the bench for another grueling season."

Rick was not consoled. "But I wanted to practice the flea-flicker! Check it out: You take the handoff, toss it back to me, and I hit Cavanaugh with a fifty-yard bomb!"

I had to laugh. "You couldn't throw a ball fifty yards if you swallowed a booster rocket off the Space Shuttle."

The coach rolled his eyes. "There's that famous honesty that makes people love you so much, Wallace."

"Well, how about an extra workout tonight?" Rick persisted.

"Can't," I said. "I've got to paint the garage door."

"Can't you get out of it?" wheedled the quarterback.

I dug in my heels. "It's just me and my mom. If I don't do it, who will? Unless"—I popped a sly grin—"you guys want to come and help."

"Not me!" chorused everybody.

"Come on," I coaxed. "Last year it took ten minutes."

"Because you bamboozled half the team into painting with you," Cavanaugh pointed out.

"Not bamboozled," I said. "The guys all knew what they were getting into."

"Great," complained Rick. "First you're on detention, and now we have to paint your stupid garage door if we want to have a flea-flicker. It's the icing on the gravy!"

I should probably explain about Rick-isms. Our quarterback had a way with words—the wrong ones.

He could take two perfectly normal expressions and wind them together like a pretzel. *The icing on the gravy* was probably supposed to be *the icing on the cake*, but Rick got mixed up with the idea that something extra could be described as *gravy*.

I had them hooked, so I reeled them in. "Come by right after practice," I invited. "I bought extra brushes for the whole offense."

There were groans of resignation from the team.

Coach Wrigley waved to Fogelman on the sidelines. "All right, he's coming." He turned to me. "Get out of here, Wallace. Go serve your time."

# Enter...
# RACHEL TURNER

*Dear Julia Roberts,*
*You are my favorite actress. Were you involved in drama when you were in seventh grade? If yes, was it tough to be a serious actress in middle school? It sure is for me. Sometimes I think I'm the only one working while everyone else is goofing off or flirting. Am I being unreasonable here? Have you ever flirted with a guy while making one of your movies? Don't feel bad if the answer is yes. You can do whatever you want because you're so famous. But student actors should have to concentrate harder, right? . . .*

It was a long letter. I told her everything—about how I knew that acting was going to be my real career. Ever since my third-grade play, *Land of the Butterflies*. All the other kids rushed off the stage screaming when Justin Kidd, the gypsy moth, threw up all over his cardboard wings (gross). I alone held my place among the giant construction-paper flowers, hugging my caterpillar costume tight and holding my breath until I passed out. Even at eight years old, I was the only one who understood—the show must go on! I'm sure Julia knew exactly what I was talking about.

Okay, I realized that Julia probably wasn't going to read this personally. When I write to movie stars, all I ever get back is an autographed picture or a postcard, or whatever they send to their fans. It just felt good to be communicating with Julia Roberts—you know, actress to actress.

"*Ow!*"

Trudi Davis elbowed me in the ribs. My pen clattered to the gym floor, but I held on to all four pages of Julia's letter and jammed it into my book bag.

"Look," Trudi whispered. "Know who that is?"

Mr. Fogelman, the director of our play, had just come in.

"Not him!" Trudi hissed. *"Him!* The kid toweling off his hair."

I shrugged. "Some eighth grader. Why? Should I know him?"

"That's Wallace Wallace," Trudi whispered.

"It can't be," I said sarcastically. "Where are his bodyguards?" No offense to the football hero (I'd never even met him). But if you weren't sick of hearing about last year's championship yet, you obviously didn't live in Bedford.

Trudi ignored my humor. "He's *hot.*"

I rolled my eyes. "Every time you're about to make an idiot out of yourself over some guy, it usually starts with the words 'He's hot.' That's warning sign number one."

"Well, he is!" she insisted. "Look!"

And actually, Trudi had a point. I'd always thought football players were neckless wonders with muscles that went all the way up to the tops of their heads. But Wallace was almost slim, and really good-looking in a boy-next-door kind of way.

"His hair's too short," I murmured just to prove nobody's perfect.

"Too long," Trudi corrected. "When you're clipped that close, you should probably buzz it all off and go for the bald look. A lot of athletes do that."

That's when it dawned on me. "This is fantastic. I'll bet the whole school will come out for the performance when we spread the word that Wallace Wallace is working with us."

"Don't count on it," warned Trudi. "Cool guys never go in for drama. If you want to act, you better do it for pure art, because guy-wise, it's the Doofus Patrol. See?" she added as Nathaniel Spitzner walked up to us.

Nathaniel stared in horror at Wallace. "What's *he* doing here?"

"What's wrong with a little fresh blood in the drama club?" I asked.

"The sportos run everything at this school," Nathaniel complained. "If they take over drama, there'll be nothing left for *us!*"

"Relax," I soothed. "The play is totally cast; we've all got our parts. Wallace is probably here to work on set design or something."

Mr. Fogelman propped himself up on the edge of the stage. "Sorry I'm late, everybody. Let's get started."

I knew it would take a few minutes to hand out scripts, so I figured this was a good time for the president of the drama club (me) to welcome the newcomer. I approached Wallace. "Hi, Wallace, I'm Rachel. Are you here to work on props?"

He looked straight into my eyes. "No."

I frowned. "Set design, then?"

"No."

"Lighting?"

"Fogelman said to come to the gym at three-thirty," Wallace told me. "This is the first I've heard about a play."

"You should sign up," I persisted. "Mr. Fogelman adapted the book just for our school. He's directing it personally!"

"What book?" he asked without much interest.

"An award winner," I said proudly. "*Old Shep, My Pal.*"

He groaned as if he had a bad stomachache.

I was kind of torn. I knew Wallace would be a great advertisement for our play. But I wasn't about to let him make fun of us.

"Mr. Fogelman is a real professional writer, you know. He even had a play produced in New York once."

"If he's the next Shakespeare," Wallace challenged, "how come he's teaching middle school in Bedford?"

I stared at him. "That's *rude*!"

"No it isn't." He looked me squarely in the eye again. "It's the truth."

"Rachel," called Mr. Fogelman, "we're starting." To Wallace he added, "You can go when you've written a proper review of *Old Shep, My Pal*. Prove to me you've read the book at least."

I joined the cast in the circle of chairs. Trudi grabbed my arm, digging her painted fingernails into my wrist. "What's he like?"

"He's like a guy serving detention," I replied, "and he isn't really thrilled to be here."

"Yeah, but did he say anything about *me*?"

"That's warning sign number two," I whispered back.

She giggled. You couldn't insult Trudi Davis. She had a hide like a rhinoceros.

There was no feeling quite like the first day of rehearsal. To take simple words on paper and bring them to life was a fantastic challenge. It was like the birth of a new baby (I'm only guessing here).

Of course, you can't have a performance on the first day. You have a staged reading. We all gathered in a circle with our scripts, and went through the entire play with each actor saying his (or her) lines. Okay, some of the cast was fooling around a little. There was a lot of laughing when Leticia Ogden choked on her gum, and when Vito Brundia read "What can this dog do?" as "What is this, *dog-doo*?" Even Mr. Fogelman had a pretty good laugh at Vito's expense. That's part of the fun of drama.

The only person who found no humor in the situation was Wallace Wallace. Mr. Fogelman stuck him right in our circle, hoping our reading would inspire his book report (Mr. Fogelman dreams in Technicolor). In fact, as the reading went on, I paid less and less attention to my part, and began concentrating on the paper in front of Wallace, who was right next to me.

This is what he wrote:

> The Lamont kids, Corey, Lori, Morry, and Tori, are always fighting. But when they find a dog that has been run over by a motorcycle, they all agree to nurse him back to health. They call him Old Shep, since he's a German shepherd. Then, just when it looks like Old Shep is going to get better, he dies. This could have easily happened way back on page one when the motorcycle got him, but then this book would never have existed. What a shame.

"Pssst!" I hissed. "Cross that out!"

He grinned at me (nice teeth for a football player).

I pointed to the last line. "That's not a review. That's mean."

"But true." He gave me the teeth again.

"No, it's not—"

"Rachel," came Mr. Fogelman's voice.

I looked up to find that I was the center of attention.

Trudi kicked me under my chair. "It's your line!" she whispered.

I grabbed my script and began flipping pages, but I was hopelessly lost.

I'm not a tattletale, but this was all Wallace's fault (sort of).

"It's because of him," I accused. "He's writing a terrible review." I caught a wild-eyed look from Wallace, like he couldn't believe I was ratting him out.

Mr. Fogelman's brow clouded up like a thunderhead. He stomped over and scanned the paper.

"This is unacceptable!" He frowned. "It's not a review; it's a plot summary, and not a very nice one at that."

"It proves I read the book," Wallace pointed out.

"You read the *words* but not the *meaning*," Mr. Fogelman insisted passionately. "The rich themes, the wonderful characters—"

"I hated the characters, Mr. Fogelman."

"You'd better be careful," warned the director. He indicated the cast (us) with a sweep of his hand. "I'll have you know you're talking to Corey, Lori, Morry, and Tori right here."

"I'm Tori," Trudi piped up. "Awesome touchdown last year. Is that a real Giants windbreaker? I've never seen one of these up close before." She stuck her elbow in my face and reached over to brush his arm. "Ooh, nice material."

Nathaniel rolled his eyes. "Give me a break!"

Wallace looked earnestly around the circle. "I've got nothing against you guys. I just didn't like the book, okay?" He stood up. "Well, thanks for—uh—having me—"

"Oh, you'll be seeing us all again," announced Mr. Fogelman. "On Monday, right after school."

You could almost see the stubborn streak rise out of the creep's spine, straighten his neck, and come forward to stiffen his jaw. "I've got football practice."

The teacher shook his head. "Not anymore. Not until you complete the work I assigned you."

"But, Mr. Fogelman," Trudi piped up, "Wallace is really important to the Giants. You know, last year—"

"I know all about last year." The director cut her

off. He looked at his watch. "We'll meet back here on Monday. That includes you, Wallace."

"Hey, Rach!"

I wheeled. My brother, Dylan, was running toward Trudi and me.

"Careful!" I cried as he raced across Bedford Avenue without a glance to the left or right (part fearless; part stupid).

He was short for a ten-year-old, so his enormous book bag very nearly dragged along the pavement as he panted up.

"Didn't anybody ever teach you to look both ways before you cross the street?" I snapped.

"Not in middle school," Dylan gasped, catching his breath. It was the biggest thrill in his life that the fifth graders had been moved out of Bedford's three elementaries, so he could go to the same school as his older sister.

"How's it going, D-man?" grinned Trudi.

"Never mind that!" Dylan exclaimed, as if he had no time for small talk. "The guy you just walked out of the gym with—wasn't that Wallace Wallace?"

"Yeah? So what?"

"*The* Wallace Wallace? The football player?"

"No, one of the other ninety-five guys named Wallace Wallace in this town!" I said sarcastically. "What's the big deal?"

"Well, what did you say to him?"

Trudi glared at me. "Tell him, Rachel. You got the poor guy in trouble with Mr. Fogelman."

"At least I didn't kiss up to him like you did," I snorted.

Trudi shrugged. "He's so cool."

"Warning sign number three," I intoned.

"I can't believe you know him!" Dylan enthused. "He's practically in the NFL!"

"Know him?" Trudi repeated. "D-man, your sister and I—we're hooked up. Actresses always hang with the 'in' crowd."

Actresses? I hope she wasn't talking about herself.

"Wow!" breathed Dylan. "Remember the big touchdown last year?"

"Don't you think it's time we all found something else to think about?" I suggested. "For instance, do you know what the school play is going to be this semester?"

But Dylan was already running down the sidewalk, backpack bouncing with each step. "Hey, Mark! Guess who my sister's best friends with!"

# Enter...
# WALLACE WALLACE

**I** **APPLIED THE FINAL** brushstroke to the garage door. "See? What did I tell you? Fourteen minutes flat."

Eleven Giants were there helping me paint. The guys never let me down when it came to jobs around the house.

"*Now* can we practice the flea-flicker?" asked Rick, brushing at a paint stain on his jeans and making it worse.

Cavanaugh jumped up. "Good idea." He always showed up at my place out of team solidarity, but he never touched a paintbrush, or a hedge clipper, or a broom. My ex–best friend wasn't crazy about me *or* the idea of helping me out.

My mother rounded the corner of the garage. "Great job, boys," she approved. "There's juice and soda in the kitchen if you're thirsty."

Feather led the stampede into the house, Cavanaugh bringing up the rear with his famous slouch. That slouch was almost as much a trademark as his super-long blond hair.

"Come back!" cried Rick. "We don't have time! The sun'll be down in forty-five minutes!"

I laughed. "Forget trying to control those guys where their stomachs are concerned."

Rick started for the door. "You hit the nail right on the hammer," he muttered.

Mom took the brush from my hand and smoothed out a bubble in the paint. "You know, I probably could have managed on my own, Wally. You don't have to call in the entire team every time a fuse needs changing."

I shrugged. "I like to do my share."

She whistled through her teeth, which was the signal that she had something on her mind. I waited.

"I've been mulling over this problem of yours at school," she began finally. "I think I've come up with a solution."

"Me, too," I replied. "What if there's an earthquake

this weekend, and a giant crack opens up, and Fogelman falls in?"

Mom pretended to consider this. "Not bad. But just in case that doesn't happen, why not try it my way?"

"I'm not going to lie." It was an old song I'd been singing all my life, and she was used to it.

"You don't have to," she said quickly. "Just write a serious paper on exactly why you think *Old Shep, My Pal* isn't any good. No wisecracks, no sarcasm, just a simple, solid essay. It's the man's favorite book, Wally. If you insult it, you're making fun of him."

"Anybody who likes that waste of toilet paper deserves to be made fun of," I observed.

"That's exactly the attitude that's been getting you in trouble," she reminded me.

I sighed.


I knew something was wrong the minute I stepped into the locker room on Saturday. The usual pregame chatter died all at once, like someone had pulled the plug.

I tossed my duffel onto the bench. "What is this, Joe's Funeral Parlor?"

Feather put a sympathetic arm around my shoulder. "Listen, Wallace, before my dad sees you—"

Too late. Coach Wrigley rounded the corner, eyes shooting sparks. "Hello and good-bye, Wallace. Get out of my locker room."

Honestly, I thought he was joking. "What are you talking about, Coach?"

"Detention is what I'm talking about!" roared Wrigley. "You're still on it!"

"Not on Saturday."

The coach shook his head. "School rules. If you're on detention, you can't play on a team, join a club, or go on a field trip—even on weekends."

Did you know that a school has more power than the government? I mean, it was *Saturday*, not even a school day! How could Fogelman have this much control over my life? I was so stunned that all I could manage was a very feeble "No kidding."

And if you think *I* was upset—

"Hey!" Rick was framed in the doorway. He dropped his helmet with a clatter. "Detention was *yesterday*!"

Cavanaugh shook his head. "This is terrible, Jackass Jackass." And when nobody was looking, the rat *winked* at me. I was the only one in the locker room who knew how much my ex–best friend was enjoying this.

"It stinks, Dad," put in Feather. "Fogelman's got it in for Wallace."

"That's *Mr.* Fogelman to you, pal," his father corrected him.

"But can't you talk to him?" Feather pleaded. "Get him to go easy. It's out of Wallace's hands."

"Wallace's hands aren't the problem," Wrigley snarled at me. "It's his mouth that keeps getting him into trouble."

"I can't believe we painted your garage door for nothing!" Rick complained. "How can we try out my new trick play if you're not even in the game?"

"The flea-flicker?" I managed, still in shock.

"This one's even better," he assured me. "Check it out: You take the handoff, but instead of running, you look for me to go deep. Then you hit me for the surprise touchdown."

"That's why you became a quarterback," I pointed out. "You couldn't catch a cold."

"Well, we'll never know *now*, will we?" Rick seethed.

The coach put a friendly arm around my shoulder. "I've got some advice for you, kid. A lot of people think football is played on the field."

"You mean it isn't?" What was he talking about?

"Look around you. Feather's on an all-celery diet to slim down and speed up. Wilkerson sleeps with a football to learn to hang on to it. Falconi's trying to memorize the playbook so he doesn't have to invent something new on every snap. These battles don't have a down and distance. But they're battles that will help our team. And now you've got one, too. It's your job to get off detention."

"But Mr. Fogelman won't—"

Coach Wrigley held up his hand. "Mr. Fogelman is *your* problem. Now, get lost. And don't come back till you've straightened out your life."

The door closed, and I was outside the stadium for the first time ever on a football Saturday. It felt like being dead. I could see my life going on all around me, but I was a nonparticipant.

Okay, so I wasn't a football nut like Feather or Cavanaugh, and certainly nowhere near to being a maniac like Rick. But I liked the game, enjoyed the physical challenge, and I had a lot of friends on the team. How could all that be over just because I wasn't psyched about *Old Shep, My Pal*? I mean, wasn't this supposed to be a free country?

I thought back to the coach's words. *Could* I get myself off detention? Of course I could. If I was my dad, the words would have flowed like sap from a maple tree: *This is the greatest book ever written. I wish I could give it ten more awards. I cried at the heartbreaking ending.* By the time Dad was through, he and Zack Paris would have been old friends. They might even have been Green Berets together in "the 'Nam."

I gagged—I just couldn't do it. It went against everything I believed in to say one nice word about such a lousy book. No way—not for football—not for anything!

"Where are you going?"

A high-pitched voice jolted me out of my reverie. This little kid stepped into my path like he was a cop, stopping a fleeing bank robber.

I'm no bully, but I wasn't in the best of moods either. "I'm going home," I said wearily. "Get out of my way."

The kid seemed genuinely horrified. "But what about the game?"

I softened. Because of that fluke touchdown last year, I had *fans*, believe it or not, among some of the little kids around town.

"I can't play," I explained patiently. "I'm on detention."

"Detention? During football season?"

"Fogelman wouldn't care if it was the last minute of the Super Bowl," I mumbled.

The runt started. "Mr. Fogelman? That's Rachel's director!" I must have looked blank, because he went on, "My sister, Rachel. You know—your friend."

I ran down a mental list of everyone I knew. There were no Rachels.

"You know," he insisted again. "The girl from the play."

"Oh. *That* Rachel." What a friend. If it wasn't for my friend Rachel, I might not even be on detention anymore. Although, to be honest, Mr. Fogelman probably would have read my review even if dear Rachel hadn't squealed on me.

"I'm Dylan, Rachel's brother." The way the kid said it, you'd think he was announcing himself as the Grand Duke of Luxembourg. "Do you want me to ask her to put in a good word for you?"

"I think Rachel's already put in enough words for me," I assured him. "So why don't you go and enjoy the game?"

The tragedy on his face was kind of flattering. "It won't be the Giants without Wallace Wallace!"

In spite of myself, I laughed out loud. "The bench will really miss me."

* * *

The Giants lost on Saturday, and my phone started ringing at about five in the afternoon. Where was I? What happened? Why wasn't I at the game?

"Mom, why don't you answer the phone for a while?"

"Well, okay, Wally," she agreed, "but I'm going to have to tell people you're not here. And that wouldn't exactly be true, would it?" She always knew how to get to me.

"Forget it," I mumbled. The phone was ringing again.

So I reprogrammed our answering machine: *"Hello. This is Wallace Wallace. If you're calling to find out why I wasn't at the game today, it's because I'm on detention. Anyone else can leave a message at the beep."*

That brought me through the weekend okay. But on Monday morning I was mobbed in the school yard. It was always the same stuff. Where was I? Why didn't I play? And how could I sit by and watch the Giants get creamed by a last-place team? I was tempted to step into my locker and pull the door shut behind me.

No way was I going to get stuck in the crush of people at the front entrance. A few minutes before the bell rang, I climbed in through the bathroom window.

And just when I thought things couldn't get any worse, they did. There, combing his ridiculously straight, ridiculously long, ridiculously blond hair, was my ex–best friend.

Cavanaugh smiled sweetly. The guy had an uncanny ability to look like an angel while he was cutting you to pieces. "Well, if it isn't Doofus Doofus," he said with all the charm of a cobra. "We missed you on Saturday. Our whole bench was out of balance. We need your weight to anchor it firmly to the field."

"You sound like you're happy about losing," I accused.

He shrugged. "*I* scored a couple of touchdowns."

That was classic Cavanaugh. The team and everybody on it could go hang, so long as he looked good. That's why the events of last year's championship game stuck in his throat so badly. It was Cavanaugh who was officially credited with the fumble, since his face made him the last Giant to touch the ball before I pounced on it for the win. I guess the guy took a lot of grief from people about playing goat to my hero. Cavanaugh had never really forgiven me for that, and I personally wasn't holding my breath for his forgiveness.

"Stop combing," I seethed. "You're driving me crazy."

"It's tough to be me." He smiled, pocketing his comb. "Every day is a good hair day." His grin never wavered. "So, Doofus Doofus, I have to tell you about this fantastic book I've been reading."

"I didn't know you could read," I muttered.

"It's called *Old Shep, My Pal*," he continued airily. "By Zack Paris. What a genius! You'd have to be a complete idiot not to love this masterpiece."

I glared at him. "All right, enough. You know why I'm on detention. Who told you?"

"A little birdie. But I know something nobody else does."

"What's that?" I growled.

"You," he chortled. "So if Fogelman is waiting for you to change your mind, this is going to be the longest detention in the history of school."

I bristled. "Not necessarily!"

"Shame, shame." He wagged a finger at me. "If you don't lie to anyone else in the world, you shouldn't lie to yourself either."

The bathroom door burst open, and in panted a fat, greasy kid with a tape recorder stuck out in front of his stomach like a hood ornament.

Cavanaugh grinned. "Make way for the press."

Parker Schmidt, alias Porker Zit, was a reporter

for the Bedford Middle School *Weekly Standard*—the only reporter. He was also the editor, publisher, printer, and delivery boy—everything except the fact checker. They didn't have one of those, which explained why the *Standard* was full of *mis*information, *dis*information, and *un*information. It was a big joke around school that the *Standard*'s motto was *If we don't mess it up, we make it up.*

"I thought I saw you climbing in here," Parker wheezed, out of breath. "I have some questions for you, Wallace, about the Giants game."

I indicated my ex–best friend. "You're in luck. We've got the captain of the team right here."

But he ignored Cavanaugh as if he wasn't there. "Why don't you just come out and admit the big cover-up?"

Parker thought he worked for *60 Minutes*.

"Yeah? What am I covering up?"

"A career-ending injury," the reporter accused.

"That's it!" crowed Cavanaugh. "He's developed a chronic charley horse of the butt!" He shook his head. "This could keep you out of the Benchwarmers' Hall of Fame, Doofus Doofus."

"Cut it out!" I snapped. "He's going to believe you and print it!"

Parker took another wild guess. "There's a personality conflict between you and Coach Wrigley! Or maybe you think you're just too good to play for a middle school team."

Cavanaugh decided to be helpful. "Hey, Porker, why don't you ask Doofus Doofus why he's spending so much time with Mr. Fogelman lately?"

"Shut up—" I began.

But Parker jumped all over that. "What's your English grade, Wallace?"

"None of your business!" I seethed.

"I can find out, you know. I've hacked the code on the office computer."

"It's an *incomplete*!" cackled my ex–best friend. "And you know why—?"

I threw my book bag at him, but he ducked, and it hit Parker, knocking the tape recorder out of his hand. I lunged at Cavanaugh, but he danced out of my grasp.

"Still the lousy tackler." He laughed, and bolted out the door.

I chased him all the way to homeroom.

## The Bedford Middle School
## Weekly Standard

# "Gimme an A or I Won't Play!"
## Superstar Holds Out for Better Grades

by Parker Schmidt, Staff Reporter

In these days of sports agents and multimillion-dollar deals, Bedford Middle School's brightest star has gotten in on the game of high-stakes contract negotiation. Only instead of a fat paycheck, Wallace Wallace is demanding a fat report card.

The Standard has learned from a reliable source that Wallace, the hero of last year's Giants, has refused to play for this year's team until Mr. Fogelman brings his English grade up from an *incomplete*.

Wallace himself refused to respond to the allegations. When pressed, he became violent and attacked this reporter with a heavy book bag, causing a severe sprain of the right index finger, and numerous scrapes and abrasions to an expensive tape recorder.

Mr. Fogelman was unavailable for comment. . . .

# Enter...
# RACHEL TURNER

**I THOUGHT I WAS** going to drop dead when I walked into rehearsal Monday afternoon. There it was, the big wooden scenery board that was going to be designed to look like the Lamont house. Right across the top, someone had spray-painted: OLD SHEP, DEAD MUTT.

It was so awful that it made me feel sick. It showed absolutely no respect for the play, the actors, the director, the scenery painters, the book—

Beside me, Trudi brayed a laugh right into my ear. "Old Shep, Dead Mutt! Yeah, that's funny!"

"Well, I don't think so," I said with feeling. Who was mean enough to do a rotten thing like this?

I stopped myself just as I was about to blurt out Wallace's name. I'd already blown the whistle on him once. And anyway, I didn't have to. Nathaniel Spitzner beat me to it.

"Wallace Wallace did it! It must have been him! He's the only one who hates *Old Shep, My Pal*!"

"Shut up, bigmouth!" snapped Trudi.

"Calm down, everyone," ordered Mr. Fogelman. "I won't have anyone accused without proof. We'll ask Wallace when he gets here."

"I'm here now" came a voice from behind us.

Our cast parted to give Wallace a view of the scenery board, and Mr. Sensitivity laughed out loud. Only Trudi (suck-up) laughed with him.

And then he stopped laughing, and an angry look came over his face. "You think *I* did this!" he exclaimed.

"Did you?" asked Mr. Fogelman.

"No!"

"He's lying!" yowled Nathaniel. "I saw him climbing in the bathroom window! I'll bet he snuck into the gym with a paint can!"

Wallace shrugged. "What's the big deal, anyway? It's painted, not carved into solid rock like Mount Rushmore."

"He's right," pointed out Kelly Ramone, who was in charge of set design. "It won't be hard to paint over it."

"We shouldn't have to paint over it," I put in darkly. "It's not supposed to be there."

"I agree," Wallace said to me. "And I repeat: I had nothing to do with it."

You know, I honestly would have forgiven him if he'd just come out and admitted that he did it because he was angry about his detention. Everybody understands what it's like to feel frustrated. But how can you sympathize with a guy who just stands there, right after he's practically been *proven* guilty, and won't own up? He obviously didn't take responsibility for the things he did. Look how he had misled poor Parker Schmidt. There wasn't one word about detention in that newspaper article. Wallace had managed to convince Parker that he was such a football star that he didn't have to earn his grades like everybody else. That's the whole problem with athletes. They get treated like gods, and it goes to their heads.

Wallace pulled a few sheets of paper from his backpack, and handed them to the director. "I did this review over the weekend. I was hoping maybe you could read it right away, and I could catch the second half of football practice."

Mr. Fogelman started to read. I could tell right off the bat that it wasn't a howling success when I caught sight of the title: "Eleven Reasons Why *Old Shep, My Pal* Is a Terrible Book." Sure enough, there it was on Mr. Fogelman's face, his Wallace expression: red neck, worry lines, wide eyes magnified behind his glasses, and a thick, bulging vein in his forehead.

"What is this?" he barked.

Wallace kept his cool. "Since you wouldn't accept my honest opinion of the book, I figured you wanted me to give you the reasons I feel that way."

"Well, they aren't *valid* reasons!" growled Mr. Fogelman. "Look at number one: 'The characters are unrealistic.' That's not true! Why, I feel like I've known the Lamont kids all my life. They're as real to me as you are."

"I hope not," Wallace replied earnestly. "I know for a fact that I've never said anything as stupid as, 'Great heavens, this dog has suffered an injury!'"

"That's not in the book!" snapped the director.

Vito's hand shot up. "Actually, Mr. Fogelman, yes it is. It's my first line after we discover Old Shep in the road."

I checked my script, and so did Mr. Fogelman. Sure enough, there it was.

may be a little old-fashioned," Mr. ___ admitted. "The book was published in ___ es, what's he supposed to say? We have to ___ dience know he's found the dog."

___ ce shrugged. "Not 'Great heavens.' How about something normal like 'Hey!' or 'Look at this!' or even 'Check it out!'? That's how people talk."

I could feel the hair on the back of my neck standing up straight. The nerve of this guy, this *football player*, telling us what to do with our play! And not just us; Mr. Fogelman, a real professional writer!

Vito spoke up. "So you think we should change the line to 'Check it out, this dog has suffered an injury'?"

Wallace looked disgusted. "Why do you have to say anything? The audience has eyes, you know. They can see an injured dog. So if the guy says, 'Check it out,' and he's looking at the dog, it's obvious what he's talking about. That's the main reason the Lamont kids are so phony. They never shut up."

"Why should we listen to you?" sneered Nathaniel. "What do you know about plays?"

"Nothing," Wallace replied. He said it proudly, as if being interested in the theater was something to be ashamed of. Maybe that was an athlete thing, too. I'll bet Wallace was going to be a celebrity for painting

OLD SHEP, DEAD MUTT on the scenery. That's just the kind of stunt his football buddies would look up to.

Mr. Fogelman handed Wallace back his latest paper. "This is unacceptable. Your detention is not canceled. And I'd better not find out that you had anything to do with that act of vandalism. Now, the rest of us have a rehearsal to run."

"Mr. Fogelman," piped up Vito, "can I do my first line the way Wallace said? I like it better that way."

I'm positive our director was dying to say no. But his face twisted into a strangled smile, and he replied, "Certainly. I'm the kind of director who believes that a play belongs to its actors. None of you should ever be shy if you have suggestions."

Trudi's hand shot up. "I've got a bunch of lines I hate, too. Can I get Wallace to fix them up?"

This time, Mr. Fogelman's smile didn't really come off that well. "Uh—"

But Trudi was already waving her script under Wallace's nose. "See here where I have to say, 'Sweet little doggie, we shall nurse you back to health'? Pretty lame, huh?"

"It stinks," Wallace agreed.

"So?" Trudi prompted. "What should I say instead?"

Wallace looked to Mr. Fogelman for permission.

This time our director's vein was bulging even more than usual. "Go ahead," he muttered.

Wallace turned back to Trudi. "Try 'Easy, pup, you're going to be just fine.'"

"That's great!" shrieked Trudi, writing it onto her script. "Now, how about here on page seven—"

"That's enough rewriting for one day," Mr. Fogelman decided.

*Dear Julia,*

*It's me again, Rachel Turner. I know you haven't answered my last letter yet, but I had a couple more questions I wanted to ask. Do you ever have anyone hassle you while you're acting? Let's say you're shooting a movie, and some really good-looking guy is hanging around the set—like Leonardo DiCaprio, or maybe Brad Pitt. He isn't acting in the movie; he's just there because maybe he got in trouble with the studio, and they're making him stay, like a detention. I know movie stars don't get detentions. But I've got a real problem here, so please keep reading . . .*

"Rachel," my mom called. "Go get Dylan for dinner."

I stuffed my letter into a drawer to finish later. "Aw," I groaned, "he doesn't even listen to you. What makes you think he'd listen to me?"

"Because if he doesn't, his chamber of horrors is going out the window, and he's going with it."

She wasn't kidding about the chamber of horrors. It was written right on his bedroom door, in letters dripping with blood. I hated going in there. Sweet little Dylan always had plenty of (sick) surprises for intruders, like a spider the size of a dinner plate, a true-to-life plastic skeleton that would wish you "Good evening" if you got too close, and fake trailing cobwebs (or maybe they were real. Dylan wasn't much of a housekeeper).

I knocked tentatively on the toxic waste sign. "Dylan. Dinner."

"Come on in, Rach."

I shuddered. "Do I have to?"

The door opened, and he grabbed my arm and pulled me inside. Actually, the chamber of horrors wasn't so bad this time. There was a lot of football stuff amid the mummies, vampire bats, and boa constrictors. In the place of honor on the night table (beside the disembodied hand), sat an eight-by-ten photograph from last year's championship. It was

Wallace Wallace, the hero, flying through the air, his body parallel to the ground, diving onto the ball for the winning touchdown. That stupid picture was displayed in every dry cleaner and doughnut shop in Bedford, even now, almost a year later.

I delivered my message. "Dinner's ready."

"Did you talk to Mr. Fogelman?" Dylan asked eagerly.

"I talk to him every day," I replied, purposely misunderstanding.

"You know what I mean," he insisted. "About getting Wallace off detention."

I sighed. "It's not up to me, Dylan. Wallace Wallace *belongs* on detention. Detention was *invented* for people like him."

"Well, couldn't you get him, like, a suspended sentence? Or a delay until after football season?"

I rolled my eyes. "If Wallace wanted to be back on the team, he could do it in two seconds. He won't write his paper. He doesn't even try anymore. He's stopped bringing a pen to the gym. He's too busy bugging people, anyway."

Dylan stuck out his jaw. "How?"

"By interrupting our rehearsals."

"What do you mean interrupting?" he persisted.

I swallowed hard, trying to be fair. "He makes—suggestions."

He stared. "What kind of suggestions?"

"On how to make the play better."

*. . . Julia, you should have seen him! He couldn't believe that his so-called idol could have anything to add to a play. I know you have a brother, too. But since he's also a famous actor, I'll bet he's a lot more supportive of your life's work. You're lucky.*

*But to get back to this guy, the one who's been messing with our play (his name is Wallace). Here's the thing—I don't know what burns me up more; that this jock, who spray-painted OLD SHEP, DEAD MUTT on our scenery, is changing our script, or that his ideas are actually (it kills me to say this) pretty good.*

*Your #1 fan,*
*Rachel Turner*

# Enter...

# TRUDI DAVIS

**WHEN I SAW** the yellow Post-it note, *It's here,* stuck to the door of my locker, I headed straight for the library. Mrs. McConville was so cool. She always let me be the first to read the new issue of *Teen Dazzle* magazine, even before it got catalogued into the computer.

I sat down at a research table and flipped through the pictures of clothes I couldn't afford and makeup my parents wouldn't let me wear. The Quiz of the Month caught my eye. It was called "Is the Perfect Boyfriend Right Under Your Very Nose?" I loved these quizzes. Of course, I cheated a little, like the time I fudged the answers so I could have every single thing in common with the national beach volleyball champion. But this time it was mega-important to do an honest job. I had a sneaking suspicion that someone pretty special was about to enter my life.

*Question 1: Do you feel your pulse quicken when you see him?* That was a tough one. Every day after classes I ran to rehearsal so fast I was, like, hyperventilating by the time I got to the gym. According to the Aerobic Workout Chart in Coach Wrigley's office, my heartbeat was the same as a normal person after twenty minutes of calisthenics. Did it get any faster when he showed up? I answered *YES AND NO*.

*Question 2: Do you think about him constantly?* Well, how much counts as constantly? I know for a fact that I thought about him nineteen times today in Spanish class alone. Figure eight periods per day, plus nights. So I probably thought about him, like, two hundred times a day, maybe more. Was that constant enough? I scribbled down *SORT OF*. They should be a lot more specific about something this important!

*Question 3: Do you find yourself overlooking his faults?* Well, that was the stupidest question of all. How could Wallace Wallace have faults?

Not only did he single-handedly win the championship for the Giants last year, but he was a dramatic genius, too! Maybe even a genius-plus! Because Zack Paris was a regular genius, and Wallace was thinking up much better dialogue for our play. Five minutes didn't go by in rehearsal without one of the actors calling out, "Hey, Wallace, have you got a better line for . . . ?" or "Can you think of a more realistic way to say . . . ?" And Wallace would always have the perfect answer.

We were all totally stumped when Leo Samuels, who played Mr. Lamont, didn't want to say, "We must look deep within our souls to accept this tragedy." But Wallace barely thought about it for a second before coming up with "Your dog died. Get used to it."

"That's not the same thing at all!" raged Mr. Fogelman.

But everybody else saw how much better it was, and Mr. Fogelman got sick of being outnumbered with only Nathaniel Spitzner on his side.

He looked daggers at Wallace. "All right, we'll try it your way."

"I don't have a way," Wallace replied honestly. "People asked my opinion, and I gave it."

When Wallace cops that confident attitude, it makes me weak in the knees. *Teen Dazzle* should be asking questions about stuff like that!

"For someone who doesn't care diddley-squat for our play," Nathaniel accused, "you sure seem to have an awful lot to say about it!"

"Hey." Wallace stood up. "I'm not even supposed to *be* here."

"Well, if you'd write your paper, you wouldn't be!" exclaimed the teacher.

And so on, and so on, blah, blah, blah. Mr. Fogelman just couldn't see that he'd never get Wallace to write that paper. Which was another thing that was awesome about Wallace. He would stand up to anybody. And being totally gorgeous didn't hurt either. I'd love to run my hand over that buzz cut of his. I'll bet it would feel like a very soft brush. A lot of people think *nerd* when they see a short haircut, but it wasn't that way at all with Wallace. His hair was more like, if he was in a rock group, the band members would wear really thin ties. Other qualities I liked about him: his voice, his *name*—other people had two names; he only had one, but you said it twice, kind of like New York, New York, or Bora Bora. Also his posture, how everybody looked up to him, and his shoelaces. Last month, *Teen Dazzle* did an article called "Learning a Guy's Secrets from His Clothes." You can tell a lot from the way someone ties his shoelaces. I'd never get involved with a sloppy-looper, or one of those weird alternative-knot types. But Wallace's sneakers were simple, neat, and tight. I got goose bumps the first time I took a good look at them.

I was in the cafeteria line, and because I was looking down, I forgot to hold my plate steady. I guess I moved it just as the lunch lady released a humongous scoop-bomb of mashed potatoes. The load dropped past my dish, over the counter, and right onto Wallace's shoes. I was shocked. One minute the laces were there, all taut and perfect; the next they were buried in food.

Wallace and I both squatted down with napkins to clean up the mess. Our eyes locked, and it would have been pure romance if I hadn't tilted my tray, spilling just enough cranberry juice to turn the mashed potatoes pink.

As it was, I couldn't resist blurting, "Do you want to come to the mall with me this afternoon?"

I'll never forget his reply from the floor as he tried to pick up the slop:

"No."

What a great guy! On top of everything else, he was

so *nice*! After all, he could easily have said something really negative! That's when I knew it was more than my third crush of the year. This time it was, like, *love*. You know?

Rachel definitely didn't approve. "You're making an idiot out of yourself, Trudi," she informed me. "Wallace Wallace doesn't even know you're alive. If you keep throwing yourself at him, he'll probably spray-paint something on you, too: OLD SHEP, DEAD MUTT, THE SEQUEL."

"You have no proof Wallace had anything to do with that," I retorted.

"Nothing except motive and opportunity," she agreed. "Plus who else could it have been?"

"Wallace wouldn't hurt the play," I told her. "He's *helping*!"

"Just because he's killing time on his detention doesn't make him one of us," Rachel insisted.

"Yeah, well, you're wrong!" I said accusingly. "And I'll prove it."

I could hardly wait for rehearsal the next day. I was all set to talk to the whole cast and clear Wallace's name—explain what a great guy he was. Only I never got to do it. When I walked into the gym, there was a terrible ruckus going on. Mr. Fogelman was shouting, Leticia was crying, Nathaniel was pointing, and Wallace was denying. Our whole crew, stage-hands, set painters, lighting and sound people, were staring in awe up at the stage. There, dead center, was a four-foot-high ball of knots made up of every micro-phone cable, spotlight cord, and speaker wire in the drama department. They were tied tightly together by the curtain ropes.

It was the great-granddaddy of all knots, a snarl that could take years to untangle.

"Who would do such a thing?" I quavered.

And all eyes were fixed on Wallace Wallace.

# Enter...
# WALLACE WALLACE

*Old Shep, My Pal* is the best book ever!! I love it so much because it is amazing, awesome, excellent, and stupendous, and also really, really great!!! There could never be a better book to get forced to read for homework!! It is the crop of the litter!!!

No, I didn't write that. It was on the typed paper that Rick Falconi placed on my kitchen table after the Giants' second loss on Saturday.

I stared at it. "What do you expect me to do with this?"

"Hand it in!" our quarterback insisted. "You can't tell a lie, but I can. So I wrote you a review to get you back on the team. I even signed your name. See? Doesn't that look like your signature?"

"Except that there are two *L*'s in Wallace," I agreed.

He slapped his forehead. "I'll cross it out and sign it again. It doesn't have to be perfect; it just has to get you off detention."

I sighed. "Come on, Rick, there's no way a review written by you is going to look like it came from me. Fogelman would see right away that you didn't read the book. It doesn't even say anywhere that Old Shep is a dog!"

Rick looked shocked. "He is? I always thought he was a sheep."

I shook my head. "You didn't even look at the cover, did you?"

He bristled. "Hey, man, I did *writing* for you! You know how much I hate writing!"

"Look." I took a deep breath. "I wouldn't hand in somebody else's work and say it's mine, even if Fogelman would never know the difference."

Rick's face fell. "Are you sure? 'Cause Feather's working on a really classy one. And he *did* read *Old Shep, My Pal.*" He looked thoughtful. "Maybe

I should've asked him about the sheep thing."

I faced him seriously. "I hate being off the team. And I'll be back the second Fogelman gives the word. But, Rick, you've got to face facts. You're losing by four touchdowns a game. I've only scored one touchdown in my entire life."

"But we were so great last year," Rick protested. "And the only difference this year is you. It's pure logicalness."

"It's not logicalness." When you spend a lot of time with Rick, the words he invents tend to become real. "Last year we were all in seventh grade. The eighth graders made up most of our starters. Now they're in high school. The only legitimate star we've got is"— and this really hurt, but after all, the truth was the truth—"Cavanaugh."

Rick was stubborn. "Even Cavanaugh knows the team needs you. After yesterday, he said that if you'd been playing, we probably would have won."

I was taken aback. "*Cavanaugh* said that?" If there was one Giant who understood my true value to the team—benchwarming—it was my ex–best friend. I mean, he never missed an opportunity to rub it in my face. So how come I was suddenly Mr. Essential?

That rotten Cavanaugh was probably trying to

work it so that the Giants' two losses would be blamed on me.

I struggled to be patient. "Cavanaugh's just making trouble as usual. When all this is over, and I come back, Coach Wrigley is going to put me where he always puts me—the bench. And the Giants are still going to stink."

Rick got so gloomy that he didn't even try to argue. "You're never coming back," he mourned. "You're going to be on detention till the cows freeze over."

"Hi, Rick." My mom breezed through the kitchen, jingling her car keys. "Sorry about the Giants."

"Mrs. Wallace, talk to your son," Rick pleaded. "Make him see how much the team needs him."

Mom smiled sympathetically. "I'd have a better chance persuading a compass to point south. I'll be right back, Wally. I'm going to the car wash."

I jumped up. "That's okay. I'll wash the car."

She looked at me. "Are you sure you don't have something more important to do? Like writing a book review?"

"I'll wash the car," I repeated. "Rick'll help, right?"

Rick flashed his paper. "If you'll hand this in to Fogelman, I'll cut your lawn, too. I'll do anything to get you back on the team."

We were just unrolling the hose when Feather rode up on his mountain bike, a stick of celery protruding from his mouth like a cigar. He waved a piece of paper of his own. "Hey, Wallace," he mumbled. "Guess what I've got!"

I took a stab at it. "My review of *Old Shep, My Pal*?"

The celery dropped to the pavement. "How did you know?"

It was easy to maneuver a polishing rag into Feather's meaty hands. Recruiting helpers normally put me in an A-1 super-good mood, but this time I was too aggravated to enjoy it. When the car was done and Rick and Feather had headed home for dinner, I marched down the block to the Cavanaugh house.

Mrs. C. greeted me like a long-lost son. She'd never quite figured out that her little Stevie and I were no longer friends. She directed me down to the basement where Cavanaugh was busy lifting weights. Even flat on his back and sweating, he looked like he had just waltzed off the cover of *Male Model* magazine.

"Well, if it isn't Jackass Jackass," he puffed. "What can I do for you, besides a brain transplant?"

I leaned on the barbell, pressing it against my ex–best friend's chest. "I'm on to you!" I snarled down at him. "Where do you get off telling the team I would have made the difference?"

"You've put on a few pounds," he observed, gasping a little, but not nearly enough to make me feel better.

"If you think you can trick the guys into blaming *me* for their lousy season—"

Slowly, he raised the weight in spite of all my efforts. He was strong as an ox. He said, "How can you think about that when a criminal is loose at school?"

That caught me off guard. I released the barbell, and Cavanaugh racked it and sat up.

"Someone is trying to sabotage the school play," he explained pleasantly. "I've worked up a little profile for the prime suspect. It has to be someone who doesn't like *Old Shep, My Pal*, has a grudge against Mr. Fogelman, and spends a lot of time in the gym. Remind you of anybody?"

To get any hotter, I would have had to be on fire. "It isn't me!" I seethed. "And you know it!"

"Don't freak out, Jackass Jackass." He lay back down and resumed his bench-pressing. "Of course *I* realize you're telling the truth. But not everybody knows you so well. So if the teachers get the wrong idea, that could keep you off the team even longer."

In a rage, I slipped an extra twenty-five-pound plate

onto the left side of his bar. And while he was struggling to balance that, I did the same to the right side.
Now fifty pounds heavier, the bar pinned him across
the chest.

I sat down to observe him squirming his way out of
it. That was another weird thing about Cavanaugh.
He would rather spend the rest of his life trapped
under that weight than ask me for help. He pushed
and wriggled and strained and sweated, but the extra
iron was just too much for him.

"Need a hand?" I asked finally.

"No." It was barely a wheeze.

Hey, you've got to respect a guy's wishes. From the
stairs I noted that all that struggling had done nothing
to spoil his good hair day.

RESEARCH

Very Guilty ////////////////////
Sort of Guilty //////////////////
Innocent ///////////////
Other //

That information was scribbled on the back cover
of *Teen Dazzle* magazine. Trudi Davis stuck it right

in my face in the gym on Monday after school.

"What is it?" I asked her.

"My survey," she explained. "You know, on who's been doing all that stuff to the play."

If ditziness was snow, this girl would be Alaska. The only thing louder than Trudi was her nail polish.

"Sort of guilty? What does that mean?" I challenged.

"It means guilty, but only—you know—sort of."

"Well, I'm glad you cleared that up," I said sarcastically.

"Don't worry, Wallace," she soothed. "Out of the thirty-two guilties, twenty-seven said that your advice on the play is so good, they don't care what you did."

"But I didn't do *anything*!" I insisted.

"Just keep pumping out those great lines," she assured me with a smile framed by tomato-red lipstick. "The tide is turning our way. I can feel it."

I handed back her chart with a groan. "What does 'other' mean?"

"Rachel refused to answer, and Nathaniel used a word I didn't understand." She checked her notes. "Disembowelment. What does that mean?"

I sighed. "Remember the last scene in *Braveheart*?"

She winced. "Ooh, that's nasty. Well, don't sweat it. He's only one person."

I nodded. "Less if you're counting by chins."

Why was I helping the actors with their lines? Part boredom, I guess. It was something to do while I was stuck on detention. But to be honest, there was another reason. It was *so* easy. I'd listen to Zack Paris's stupid dialogue, and just say the same thing the way normal people talk. I even kind of enjoyed it—you know, the way you can't help but like bowling if it turns out you're good at it. Hey, if Zack Paris had used my dialogue, maybe *Old Shep, My Pal* wouldn't be such a lousy book, and I wouldn't be spending all my afternoons in the gym.

# Enter...
# RACHEL TURNER

Dear Julia,

Hi, it's Rachel again. I'm sorry to bother you so much, but I never thought that a simple play could get so complicated. Remember Wallace Wallace? (I know you must hear a lot of names, but probably not that many with two of the same.) In my last letter, I told you he was nothing more than a good-looking jock with an attitude. But now I'm starting to see that he's smarter than that. He's dangerous!

Not only am I positive that he's the

*culprit behind* Old Shep, Dead Mutt *and the big cable knot, but now I see all that is just a smoke screen to cover up his real plan. By pretending to help out, he's winning the confidence of the cast and crew, and making changes one by one to destroy our play. It's his revenge for getting kicked off the football team. And I'm the only one who realizes it . . .*

"That's the stupidest thing I've ever heard in my whole life!"

I wheeled to find Trudi reading over my shoulder.

"Are you crazy?" I roared. "This is a private letter!"

"You're writing to Julia Roberts about Wallace Wallace, and *I'm* crazy?"

I could feel myself blushing crimson. "When I write to famous actresses, I don't really expect them to read my letters. I just do it as a form of self-expression. It's almost like keeping a journal or a diary."

She looked unconvinced. "Do you mail them?"

"Well—yeah," I admitted.

She was shocked. "Rachel, how could you? Julia Roberts is going to think that Wallace is some kind of gangster!"

"Trudi, I know you like him," I said patiently. "But after all he's done to us, how can you take his side?"

"Because he's a gifted playwright," she said stubbornly. "Not to mention adorable, a football hero, and someone who could get us invited to all the coolest parties!"

Trudi seemed to think there was this ultra-hip "scene" out there, where rock stars, the rich and famous, and the beautiful people (but not Trudi Davis) hung out together. Oh, I'm sure it existed somewhere, but definitely not at the Bedford 7-Eleven. And I doubt you could could join it by dating a middle-school football player, even the celebrated Wallace Wallace.

I was so upset, I couldn't enjoy the evening out my dad planned for the whole family in honor of Mom's birthday. We were driving in to New York to see a real Broadway play. I'd been excited for weeks because the theater is my whole life. (Now, thanks to *Old Shep, My Pal*, I got a queasy feeling in my stomach every time I heard the word "play.")

My brother didn't make things any easier. "Why do we have to go to a dumb old play?" he whined for most of the hour-long drive. "I hate plays."

"You love the theater," my mother said in surprise. "Remember how much you enjoyed *Cats*?"

"That was before a stupid play ruined the Giants," Dylan growled, "and stuck Wallace Wallace on detention."

There it was. Wallace Wallace was following me to New York (courtesy of Dylan).

"Your hero is on detention because of his own big mouth," I said sourly. "And if Nathaniel Spitzner had his way, he'd be on death row."

My father was astonished. "You know Wallace Wallace? What's he like?"

*. . . you see, Julia? My own father, my own brother, my own best friend! If you were shooting a movie, and Brad Pitt was out to ruin it, but your agent, your manager, and your lawyer refused to believe it just because he was the great Brad Pitt, wouldn't you be really mad? That's how I feel.*

*But enough about me. What's new in your life? Any blockbuster movies in the works? Don't costar with Brad Pitt. Ha, ha. Just kidding.*

*Your fellow actress,*
*Rachel Turner*

* * *

"Wallace," Vito called the next day at rehearsal, "this speech doesn't sound natural to me."

Mr. Fogelman stepped in. "We've changed that part."

"I can't get into my character's mind," Vito insisted.

That made Nathaniel wince. "Two weeks ago, you tried out for this role to make up for an F in art. Now, suddenly, you have to get inside Morry Lamont's head?"

But Wallace was already climbing up the stairs to the stage. My back teeth were clenched so tight that I could feel the tension headache coming on. These were the moments I had come to dread the most. Fix this! Cut that! And nobody seemed to be able to stop him.

Wallace took Vito's script. "Let me see."

"No way," the director persisted. "You've already rewritten this speech. Every single word. All ten lines."

"Well, that's the whole problem," Wallace explained. "It's too long. Nobody does this much talking without something else going on."

"Like what?" Mr. Fogelman demanded.

"Something real people do," Wallace said thoughtfully. He reached around and pulled the yo-yo out of Vito's back pocket.

"Here." Wallace popped it into his hand. "Try playing with this when you give that speech. Be distracted. You're talking, but at the same time you're 'rocking the cradle.'"

The strangest feeling began to come over me. My ears burned, then roared. I started fidgeting because I couldn't keep my feet still.

"Now, just one minute!" ordered Mr. Fogelman. "There are no yo-yos in *Old Shep, My Pal*."

"It's just something for the audience to watch," Wallace insisted. "I mean, this whole play is nothing but a bunch of knuckleheads standing around talking."

My script slipped out of my clammy hands and hit the gym floor.

"That's not true!" Mr. Fogelman countered angrily. "They're nursing Old Shep!"

"And where's Old Shep?" the creep argued. "You've got a basket with a blanket in it. This is a dog play with no dog."

I was going to faint, or die, or something! I had to let it out somehow!

Mr. Fogelman chuckled. "That's just for rehearsals. Of course we'll use a stuffed animal for the performance. Old Shep's been hit by a motorcycle before the play even starts. All he has to do is lie in the basket."

"That's the biggest problem of all," Wallace told him.

And suddenly, the pressure that had been building up inside of me let go with the force of an atomic bomb.

*"OH, YEAH?!!"*

The shocked silence that followed was so total, I could hear the echo of my scream bounce off every wall in the gym.

*"Tell us, Mr. Expert!"* I howled at Wallace. *"Let's see what kind of writing talent a person gets from diving on a football! Let's hear it, since you know better than the whole drama club, better than our director who had a play produced in New York, and better than Zack Paris himself, who ONLY wrote a classic, and never fell on a football once!"*

Wallace Wallace may have been a star athlete, but I guess he'd never seen anybody go berserk before, because he looked just plain scared. I wasn't expecting that. And after all my shouting, I found myself almost at a loss for words.

"I—I'm sorry," was all I could manage. "I mean, I'm not sorry—but I'm sorry for yelling."

"Rachel's right," said Wallace, very subdued. "This is none of my business." He started off the stage.

And it would have been over—all of it!—if Vito hadn't opened up his yap.

"Wallace, don't go! We need your help! What were you going to tell us about our play?"

Wallace sighed. "It's been a very long afternoon." He turned to Mr. Fogelman. "Can I leave now? I promise I won't go anywhere near football practice."

"But you were going to tell us about a problem!" Trudi shrilled. "The biggest one of all, you said!"

The whole cast and crew started encouraging Wallace.

Mr. Fogelman held his head. "All right, let's hear it."

Reluctantly, Wallace spoke up. "I'm no expert, but this seems like common sense. In the story of *Old Shep, My Pal*, the most exciting event is when the dog gets run over by a motorcycle. And you've taken out that part before the play even starts. Which means no one gets to see any action, ever."

"This is a school play, Wallace!" exploded Mr. Fogelman. "What do you want me to do—buy a thirty-thousand-dollar Harley? Hire a stunt man to ride it? And a professional stunt dog, along with his trainer? Where do I send away for that? Hollywood?"

Inside, I was applauding, but I never said a word. I

was planning to keep my mouth shut for a good long time.

"You know, it doesn't have to be a real motorcycle," Vito put in. "My mom has an old moped she'd probably let us use."

"It doesn't matter!" Mr. Fogelman insisted. "We don't have the resources to hire a trained dog, or to train one of our own. Let's get real here, people, and do what we *can* do."

But Wallace wasn't done yet. "Mr. Fogelman, what about one of those little remote-control cars? If we attach the toy dog on top, one of the stagehands can work the remote, and the audience will see Old Shep running out into the road."

This was the craziest idea of all! Surely even an idiot could see that!

"It's brilliant!" screeched Trudi.

(Okay, maybe not a truly dedicated idiot.)

"Perfect!" Vito was shaking with excitement. "We can glue on Old Shep so you'll never see the car underneath."

Leticia nodded eagerly. "Then he crosses the street, and *bang!* The moped gets him."

"I love it!" raved Kelly. "What a great beginning! The audience will be hooked!"

I was horrified. Half the actors started volunteering their little brothers' and sisters' remote-control cars.

"Hold it, people!" The director tapped for silence, and got none. Excited chatter filled the gym. The stagehands were fighting over who would get to ride the moped; the set designers wanted to build a stop sign for where the accident would take place.

"I'll work the remote control!"

"No, I'll work the remote control!"

"*QUI-ET!!*"

Mr. Fogelman ended my brief reign as the loudest yeller in the gym. His voice was a foghorn.

"I don't want to hear another word of this," the director said sternly. "We will begin our play where Zack Paris began his book. And that's final."

"But Mr. Fogelman!" protested Trudi. "You told us that a play belongs to its actors."

"Yes," the teacher replied. "*This* play. But the kind of changes you're talking about make it some other play."

"Yeah! A better one!" exclaimed Vito earnestly.

And the babble started up again.

"Mr. Fogelman's right!" Nathaniel pleaded into the ruckus. "Let's listen to our director!"

Forget it. The gym was pandemonium. Big, affable

Vito was waving his arms and howling. Trudi's high-pitched, strident voice rang out like a policeman's whistle. Everton Wu, a tiny, shy fifth-grade stage-hand, was right in Mr. Fogelman's face, registering his protest.

But Mr. Fogelman hadn't gotten a real play produced in New York by letting himself be pushed around. He put up with the shouting for a while, and then he laid down the law.

"All right, people, listen up," the teacher commanded. "This is our play, and this is how it's going to be performed. If anybody is unwilling to do that, let me know, and I'll begin looking for your replacement."

In all the time Trudi and I had been friends (forever), I'd never seen her so angry.

I begged her to be reasonable. "The first rule of drama is to listen to the director. The director is like the *president* of the play."

"That's not true!" Her response was bitter." If you don't like the president, you can vote him out of office. But nobody ever voted for Mr. Fogelman!"

## Enter . . .

# MR. FOGELMAN

**MEMO: Talk to Coach Wrigley**

It was two weeks ago that I approached the coach in the faculty room. I felt he should hear it from me that it didn't look like Wallace would be writing his review any time soon.

He raised an eyebrow. "Wallace is a pretty straight kid. Stubborn."

I rolled my eyes. "Tell me about it."

The coach poured himself another coffee. "What exactly has he done?"

"He's pulled a smart-aleck routine over my book review project," I explained. "I thought an afternoon of detention might make my point. Now I'm getting dirty looks from students in the hall. I ordered a pizza last night, and when I gave my name, the girl on the phone said, 'You'd better let Wallace Wallace come back to the Giants.'"

Wrigley handed me a cup. "Bedford had never won anything before. Now that they're champions, they expect to compete every year. Believe me, I'm feeling the heat because we're losing."

"What do you do about it?" I asked.

"I don't order any pizzas, that's for sure."

I sat down on the couch. "And Wallace is such a good player that my detention puts you in last place?"

"Nah!" He shook his head. "If Wallace could make the difference for the Giants, I'd be all over you to give the kid a break."

"But everybody says—" I began.

"Trust me. Our lousy season has nothing to do with Wallace Wallace."

I liked Coach Wrigley. I was glad there were no hard feelings between us. I stood up. "One last thing. You know Wallace. How long do you think it'll take before he sees it my way?"

Wrigley pointed ominously out the small window. "That parking lot is paved with the bones of teachers who are still waiting for Wallace to see it their way."

**MEMO: Stay the course. Don't panic.**

Maybe I should have listened to the coach's warning. But how could I have predicted what Wallace would do to our play. I can barely *describe* it! I tried, to my wife, Jane, and I wound up sounding like a fool:

"Well, at first everybody loved him because he was a football star. Then they hated him because he spray-painted 'Old Shep, Dead Mutt' on the Lamont house. Now they love him again because he helped them punch up their lines, but they hate *me* because I won't let them use a moped to run over a stuffed dog on a toy car."

"You're under a lot of stress," she said soothingly.

"But it's *true*!" I insisted.

Trudi Davis summed it up during one of the three visits she made to my office that day. "Wallace showed us how to turn a typical yawn of a school play into something *awesome*. How can we go back to the old way?"

**MEMO: You don't have to explain yourself. You're the director.**

Rehearsals were a nightmare. The actors were depressed and demoralized, and the scenery painters didn't care anymore. When Kelly showed me the

Lamont house, it was nothing but a big, blank backdrop, with two square windows, and a rectangular door drawn in Magic Marker.

I stared at her. "That's it?"

"Yep." I could almost feel the arctic blast.

"But what about the bricks?" I persisted. "And the curtains! The shutters! The flowerpots! The trees and the ivy! What happened to the chimney? Your sketches were beautiful! This is—nothing!"

"We all talked it over," she explained, "and since you won't let Wallace turn our play into something special, what's the point of having good scenery?"

"But Wallace isn't even *in* our play!" I argued. "None of this makes any difference to him!"

**MEMO: Reason with the kids.**
On my lunch hour, I approached Leticia in the science lab. She got so agitated that she forgot to watch an experiment that had taken her two days to set up. I cornered Vito in the boys' change room, and he was just as angry. As soon I said Wallace had no authority, he turned on the hand dryer so it was impossible to hear me. It was the same thing with Leo in the gym. When I mentioned rehearsal, he shot up the rope so

fast that he set a sixth-grade record for the county. Now Wrigley wants him to quit the play and go out for gymnastics.

**MEMO: Never try to reason with kids. You'll go crazy.**

As the week progressed, my cast and crew took to coming in late, and in some cases, not showing up at all. Out of forty-five kids, I had thirty-three on Monday, only twenty-eight on Tuesday. By Wednesday, I was down to nineteen.

The frustration was mind-numbing. During my off-Broadway run in New York, my actors had been waiters and garbage collectors and revolutionaries. I had to take a taxi to Police Plaza at four in the morning to bail my leading lady out of jail. Now I knew the truth: Those were the good old days.

**MEMO: Get help from the principal.**

I left Nathaniel in charge of rehearsal, and headed for Dr. Chechik's office.

"Okay, everybody," announced Nathaniel. "Let's do Scene Two, where we bring Old Shep home."

It was an ordinary thing that could have come from any director. But the whiny, obnoxious, self-important way Nathaniel said it got under everyone's skin. I paused at the door as the actors took their sweet time shuffling up to the stage.

"Hurry up, hurry up," Nathaniel nagged.

"Let's go, people," I added.

"Wallace, I'm not too thrilled with my line here—" Vito complained.

Nathaniel cut him off. "We're not asking Wallace anymore! He shouldn't even be here."

Wallace stood up. "In that case, I'll be at football practice."

"No! You're on detention! If you leave, I'm telling!"

Trudi rolled her eyes. "Spitzner, were you born a dork, or did you have to get a degree?"

**MEMO: You don't put Nathaniel in charge of an anthill. Pretty soon the ants would all be rising up to kill him.**

I postponed my trip to the office. "That's enough." I clapped my hands. "Places, everybody."

"Hey, what's that?" asked Rachel.

I followed her pointing finger to a jump rope that hung down from the top of the tall scenery board, dangling in front of the painting of the house.

"Maybe my character snuck out last night to meet her boyfriend," said Trudi, flashing Wallace a dazzling smile. "I'm very romantic, you know."

**MEMO: Beware of hormones. You will never defeat them.**
"This isn't supposed to be here," Nathaniel said in annoyance. He grabbed the end of the jump rope and yanked.

His face radiated pure horror when he realized what was on the other end of the cord. It was a bucket that stood balanced on top of the scenery board. As it fell, it tipped over, releasing a dense cloud of black pepper right onto my actors' heads.

Trudi was the first to sneeze. But I couldn't tell who was second, because it was an epidemic of coughing and hacking and sputtering. I ran for the stage, but as soon as I got close, the spicy powder went straight up my nose. My eyes filled with water, and I stopped in my tracks, wheezing.

"Ow!" cried Nathaniel as the bucket bounced off his head. He fell, and his collision with the floor raised up another cloud of pepper. Down there, he was kicked and stepped on by the others in their mad scramble to brush themselves off and escape the airborne powder. And above the symphony of sneezes rose another sound, a deep, hearty laugh that could only have belonged to Wallace Wallace.

I tried to yell, "Can it, Wallace!" But when I opened my mouth, more pepper got in, and I ended up choking and spitting instead.

Through watery eyes, I was aware of a blurry commotion of moving shapes. As my vision cleared, I saw Wallace leading the victims one by one away from the pepper storm.

"If you wanted to help," came Rachel's raspy voice, "you could have not done this in the first place!"

After a couple of quiet days, she was back to her old self, except now she had even less patience for Wallace Wallace than I did.

At that moment, Nathaniel, who was still blinded and sneezing, struggled to his feet.

"Careful!" I cried.

He wobbled backward, and then stepped clear off the edge of the stage.

In a flash, Wallace was there. He caught the smaller Nathaniel in outstretched arms. There they were, in the pose of a groom carrying his bride across the threshold.

I was just about to lace into Wallace for planting that bucket of pepper when the entire cast and crew burst into applause and cheers.

"Bravo!"

"Nice catch, Wallace!"

"It's your best play since the touchdown!"

It dawned on me like a new day. *This* was exactly what was missing from our play! Our cast—happy, laughing, excited, united. It was the kind of enthusiasm that couldn't be manufactured.

**MEMO: Seize that energy and harness it for the good of the production.**

Well, I had to do *something*. Otherwise, we might be down to ten people at tomorrow's rehearsal, and only five on Friday. Next week, I'd have to cancel the play altogether.

I raised my hand for order. "Listen up, people. I've got something important to say."

"Mr. Fogelman," piped Nathaniel, "make Wallace put me down!"

Obligingly, Wallace dropped his arms, and Nathaniel clattered to the hard floor.

"Ow!"

"I've been doing a lot of thinking," I went

on. "Since everybody's so enthusiastic, I've decided that we should try the first scene your way."

There was dead silence, and then Trudi burst out, "You mean *Wallace's* way?"


**MEMO: They always know how to hurt you.**

It killed me to *reward* Wallace for vandalizing our play. I reminded myself that I had no proof that this had been his doing. "I mean the proposed new scene with the moped and the remote-control car to move the dog—"

I didn't get a chance to finish because pandemonium broke out. There was so much backslapping and jumping for joy that yet another cloud of pepper was raised from people's clothes and hair. That brought on more sneezing, only this time it was happy sneezing. Even Wallace looked sort of pleased, a welcome change from his usual scowl of defiance. At least he was coughing and spitting now, too, caught by his own dirty trick.

Rachel approached me, fanning away pepper with her script. "Why did you do it, Mr. Fogelman?" Her reddened eyes conveyed deep anguish. "Why?"

"I know it sounds crazy," I replied. "But I really think this is the only way."

Now who was going to convince *me*?

# Enter...

# WALLACE WALLACE

"**A**TTAWAY, GIANTS!"

"Let's go, team!"

I scrunched down into my hood in the hope that
the two noisy fans in the next row wouldn't call attention to me. I had agonized a lot over whether or not
I should go to the Giants' third game. By this time,
everyone in Bedford but the pigeons knew about
my detention and my disgrace. But that didn't stop
them from nagging: What went wrong? What are
you doing to fix it? And the everlasting Why? Why?
Why? Why? Why? Parker Schmidt called my house
so often these days that he and my mom were turning
into phone buddies.

So I was sort of in disguise. The hood of my windbreaker covered all my hair, a big muffler concealed my mouth and nose, and a headband fixed it so that only my eyes were showing. Trouble was, we were having Indian summer, and it was seventy-six degrees. I thought I was going to melt!

The Giants were doing pretty well, grinding out yardage in a tight defensive game. Cavanaugh's four field goals had given them a 12–7 lead. I watched the whole thing with sweat pouring into my stinging eyes. Underneath my layers of camouflage, I was as wet as if I'd just climbed out of a swimming pool.

But I was happy in my sogginess. The guys were having their best Saturday this year. With the ball and less than a minute to go, all they had to do was run out the clock. Once they'd won a game without me, surely Rick and the team would see that I wasn't indispensable.

"Hey, son," said the man next to me as he took off his shirt. "You look like you're having a heart attack. Why are you dressed for the North Pole?" Helpfully, he reached out, pulled off my headband and hood, and pushed down my scarf. I was out in the open.

And fate had put that little kid, Dylan, Rachel Turner's brother, a few seats away.

*"Hey, everybody!"* he shrieked in a voice that carried all through the stadium. *"Look! It's Wallace Wallace!"*

Everybody *did* look. And you could hear a gigantic *"Wal-lace"* as hundreds of people mumbled my name, passing it from tongue to tongue like trench mouth.

*"Wallace?!"*

I recognized *that* voice. It was Rick Falconi on the field, gazing up into the stands looking for me instead of keeping his eyes on—

*"The ball, Rick!"* I bellowed. *"Watch the ball!"*

The snap bounced off the side of Rick's helmet and wobbled into the backfield, where it was picked up by the biggest, strongest, slowest lineman on the other team.

*"Hit him!"* I cried.

And they did. Some of them bounced off. Those who managed to hang on were dragged seventy yards down the field by the enormous lineman. Rick, who was clamped onto an ankle, was repeatedly slapped against the turf like a flyswatter as the big kid returned the fumble for the winning touchdown.

Ouch.

The mood in the locker room was despair-minus-minus. I should have snuck home, but I felt kind of responsible for this, our third loss. And it wouldn't have been right to duck out on the team.

You could tell that Rick wanted me dead. "I refuse to see you, Wallace!" The poor guy was one extended bruise from his trip down the field attached to that runaway locomotive. "I saw you once already, and look what happened!"

I indicated my heavy clothes. "I was trying not to be noticed. But then some guy pulled down my hood."

"If you were on the field where you belong," Feather said sourly, "nobody could pull down your hood."

"And we would've won," added Rick.

"It wasn't a total disaster," I argued. "You really showed something out there. If it wasn't for that last play, you had it kicked."

"It was a disaster, all right," Rick moaned. "By any stretch of the means."

Rick-ism math: *By any stretch of the imagination* + *By any means* = *By any stretch of the means*.

Cavanaugh stepped forward, and I knew the rough ride was only beginning. "This was a close game, Wallace," he declared loudly. Because he called me Wallace, and not some nasty double nickname, I realized that his true audience was the team and not me.

"I scored twelve points, so a star like you could have gotten at least that many. We would have won by a mile!"

A chorus of grumbles bubbled up in the locker room.

"We need you on the team, not in the gym!"

"We're getting killed out there!"

"We're 0 and three!"

Silence fell as Coach Wrigley stepped out from his office. He gave me a crooked smile. "Congratulations, Wallace. I see your public hasn't forgotten you."

"Sorry, Coach," I murmured.

He clapped me on the shoulder. "It wasn't your fault. Relax. Go home. Maybe even—write a book review."

I just couldn't look him in the eye. Instead, I concentrated on the concrete floor, my sneakers, Rick's muddy cleats, Feather's open locker—

I froze. There on the shelf beside Feather's wadded-up sweat socks stood a two-pound box of ground black pepper. I had a vision of the cast and crew of *Old Shep, My Pal* coughing and sneezing in a big black cloud.

"Hey, Feather—" I hardly recognized my own voice. "What's with the pepper?"

He made a face. "It's for the celery, to disguise the taste."

"Yeah," I insisted, "but two pounds?"

"Ever eaten celery?" He snorted. "Two pounds isn't enough."

As it turned out, I wasn't the only one thinking about the attacks on *Old Shep, My Pal*. First thing Monday morning, I got called to the principal's office.

Dr. Chechik spent the first few minutes showing me his poster-size blow-up of the newspaper photograph of me scoring the winning touchdown. The next few minutes he devoted to telling me that I couldn't expect any special treatment because of it.

I kind of liked our principal. He was a straight-up guy who got right to the point. He asked if I did it, and I said no. But then he caught me off guard:

"Do you have any idea who might be responsible?"

I was stuck. I couldn't tell him my suspicions about Feather. After all, the kid had a good reason for keeping a lockerful of pepper. Besides, I'd never rat out a friend. But I couldn't lie either.

"I can't say for sure," I replied. The "for sure" made it okay.

When I left the office, my head was spinning. Why would Feather have a grudge against the play? The answer was simple. The whole Giants team was mad at Mr. Fogelman over my detention. Feather was the most obvious suspect because of the pepper. But it could also be Rick, or Kevin Wilkerson, or any of those guys who were dumb enough to believe I was a big star.

And what about Cavanaugh? He didn't want me back on the Giants, but he sure got a charge out of watching me suffer. He could be doing all this to set me up. Pinning the blame on me would guarantee that my detention would go on forever. Come to think of it, Cavanaugh seemed to know a lot about what was happening to the play. Was that because he was making it happen?

When I walked out of the office, Parker Schmidt was skulking on the bench. I'll bet he'd been hiding there ever since he'd heard my name paged over the P.A.

"I can't believe you have the nerve to come anywhere near me!" I snarled. "Especially after what you printed last time!"

He waved the slightly damaged tape recorder in my face. "Did your meeting with the principal have anything to do with your ongoing holdout from the Giants?"

What an idiot! He even sounded like his stupid articles.

But then I got an idea. For some strange reason, a lot of kids read the *Standard* and talked up Parker's columns. If I leaked to Parker that Dr. Chechik was looking into the attacks on *Old Shep, My Pal*, chances are the bad guy would read it and back off. Then I wouldn't have to take the blame anymore, and Rachel Turner could stop yelling at me. Fat chance.

So I sat him down and gave him all the facts. He looked at me suspiciously the whole time. You could tell Parker wasn't used to having a real story to write. He did most of his hard-hitting journalism on PTA fund-raisers, stuffing himself on complimentary brownies.

"That's why Dr. Chechik paged me," I finished. "He's heard about the attacks on the play, and he's determined to get to the bottom of it."

"And he needs your help," Parker concluded.

"Well, he asked me about it," I explained. "I guess that counts as helping. But the important thing is he's on the case. Got it?"

Parker patted his tape recorder. "This is a real scoop. Thanks a lot, Wallace."

As he walked away, I remember thinking maybe people were too hard on Parker Schmidt. He wouldn't make so many mistakes if more kids would take the time to answer his questions.

# The Bedford Middle School
## Weekly Standard

# Wallace Wallace, Secret Agent

by Parker Schmidt, Staff Reporter

The Standard has learned the true reason behind superstar Wallace Wallace's holdout from the Giants. The hero of last year's championship game has been recruited by Dr. Chechik to be the principal's eyes and ears in the school.

The new role is so top-secret that Dr. Chechik himself refused to acknowledge that such an arrangement has been made. There was no comment on whether or not this undercover spy work would raise the incomplete that Wallace is currently receiving in English. . . .

His responsibilities will include keeping an eye on every single one of us and reporting directly to the office. And while some may consider this job description to be "professional rat," this reporter considers it a bold step toward law and order here at Bedford Middle School.

# Enter...
# WALLACE WALLACE

**I WAS HALFWAY UP** the tree, pruning off dead branches when I saw Rick and Feather. Right on schedule. Every fall, the guys on the team came over to help me spread Lawn-Gro on the grass. It was just another chore I didn't want my mom to have to do—especially when there was an entire football team who could knock it off in two seconds. And even though one of them—maybe a close friend—was the jerk who was attacking the play, that still left a whole lot of pretty good guys who deserved the benefit of the doubt from me.

I waved. "I'm up here!"

"Hang on with two hands, Wallace!" Rick shouted up at me. "How are you going to get back to the team if you break both your necks?"

I had to laugh. "Maybe I'll just break one of my necks, and I'll still have a spare for football." I clipped off a brown twig with my pruning shears. "I'll be done with this in a few minutes. That'll give the others a chance to get here."

There was so much throat-clearing and coughing down there that I decided I'd better cut my work short. I clambered lower on the trunk and dropped to the grass at their feet. "What's going on? Are the others going to be late?"

Feather shuffled uncomfortably. "There *are* no others," he mumbled.

"Sure there are," I told him. "I asked a whole bunch of guys—all the wide receivers and at least three defensive backs."

"And did they tell you they were coming?" Rick challenged.

"No," I said. "They never do. And they always come. Where's Kevin? I figured him for the weeding. He has great eyes for dandelion spotting."

Feather cleared his throat carefully. "Kevin said if you're not on the team, he's not your gardener."

I snickered. "Come on, Feather. Where is everybody? Hiding over by the 7-Eleven?"

Rick gave me an agonized look. "You're not listening, man!"

I peered down the street in both directions. Nobody.

It must seem like I'm a pretty big idiot because it was taking me so long to clue in. But this was a leap for my mind. I'd always thought my teammates came to help because they were my *friends*. And they understood how important it was for me to pull my weight and help Mom. I never thought it had anything to do with football. Football was just how I knew them.

"It was Cavanaugh, right?" I asked. "He's behind this."

"You've got to look at it through the team's eyes," pleaded Feather, his face open and sincere. "They're getting shelled every week. Then they open up the *Standard* and read how you're holding out for better grades, or spying for Chechik."

"That's just Porker!" I exclaimed. "The guy's less than stupid! Nobody believes his stuff!"

"Maybe," shrugged Rick. "But it seems like you're not even *trying* to get back. And they think, hey, if the cake fits, eat it."

I admit it. I was bitter. "So are you guys here now

because you're my friends, or because you think you can get me to write a review of *Old Shep, My Pal*?"

"Of course we're your friends!" Feather exclaimed.

"But if you want to write the essay, that would be good, too," Rick added eagerly.

It was impossible to stay mad at those two, especially with a whole lawn that needed fertilizing.

We took turns pulling weeds and pushing the spreader back and forth across the yard. And just when we were almost done, the delivery van from Chee-Zee Pizza whipped around the crescent, and pulled into our driveway, leaving tire tracks along the corner of the lawn.

"Hey!" I yelled.

The door of the van opened, and out stepped Laszlo Tamas. Even though Laszlo was older than we were, he was in eighth grade at our school. His family was from Hungary, and he was being held an extra year in middle school to work on his English.

I think moving to Bedford from Budapest must have been a great deal, because Laszlo was always cheerful. Even when he apologized for driving over our freshly fertilized lawn, he seemed pretty happy about it.

"Oops!" He beamed. "Sorry." He brushed off his Chee-Zee Pizza uniform and shook hands with all three of us. Hand-shaking was not big at Bedford Middle School, but I guess nobody told Laszlo. To me he said, "I heard you wanted to see me."

The thing about Laszlo was that he was sixteen, and had just gotten his driver's license. You had to be sixteen to ride a moped. Now, we only needed it for thirty seconds in the opening scene of *Old Shep, My Pal*. But Fogelman was being a jerk about it, big surprise.

"Someone has to ride Vito's mom's moped in the school play," I explained, "and you're the only one who's old enough to do it. What do you say?"

"Wow! Really? *Me?*" This was just another one of those things that pleased Laszlo to pieces. He enfolded me in a giant bear hug, and shook hands again with Feather and Rick.

Rick frowned, perplexed. "Wait a minute, Wallace. How come you're lining up guys for *Old Shep, My Pal*?"

"Yeah," echoed Feather. "What's the play got to do with *you*?"

I shrugged. "Nothing, really. I'm stuck down there every day, and their rehearsals are so bad that sometimes you just have to say something. If they take it for advice, it's not my fault."

Feather was obviously suspicious. "So why are you helping? Advice isn't the same as finding a guy to ride a moped."

"It's just this once," I explained. "Otherwise Fogelman was going to ride it himself. He's so clueless, and I knew Laszlo, and what the heck—why not?"

Laszlo suffocated me with another emotional hug. "It's my honor to work with Wallace Wallace!"

"I don't like it," Rick said ominously. "I smell a fish in here somewhere."

"You don't smell a fish," I reassured him. "There's nothing to smell."

"Right," agreed Laszlo. "I'll see you at our rehearsal, Wallace."

As Laszlo got back in the van, I could see Rick and Feather watching him—and me—with narrowed eyes.

# Enter...
# RACHEL TURNER

*Dear Julia,*

*Tell your secretary thanks for the autographed picture and the application to join your fan club. I promise I'll fill it out as soon as I have time. As you know, things have been pretty busy around here, what with Wallace trying to ruin our play.*

*You know life is really bad when your friends are causing you just as much aggravation as your enemies. Have you ever had a friend who did that to you? For instance, if Brad Pitt was spoiling your*

*movie, wouldn't it only make it worse if*
*your own best friend started hitting on him?*
*There's this girl, Trudi Davis . . .*

I was in Spanish class, conjugating, when Trudi leaned over and whispered, "Harold Schwartzbaum."

Now, Spanish is not my best subject, but I knew Harold Schwartzbaum was not the verb to dance. "What about him?"

"He's the one who's been doing all those things to the play," she murmured urgently.

I was skeptical. "How do you figure that?"

"On the day of the big pepper bomb, Wendy Pappas saw him sneeze in class."

I laughed. "Harold Schwartzbaum is allergic to everything. I've never seen him when he didn't have a Kleenex attached to his face."

"Not only that," Trudi went on, "but when he heard about '*Old Shep, Dead Mutt,*' Wendy says he laughed."

"Wendy should find herself a better hobby than spying on Harold Schwartzbaum," I shot back. "Half the school laughed. *You* laughed."

"Yeah, but I know I didn't do it," she reasoned.

"Look," I cut her off. "Everybody knows who's

doing it. It's your precious Wallace Wallace."

Trudi looked at me like I had just accused the Easter Bunny of armed robbery. She folded her arms in defiance. "Then how come Wallace is trying to find out who's doing it?"

"Why? Because Parker Schmidt says he's an undercover agent?" I exclaimed. "That guy thinks *Star Wars* is a documentary! If you believe the *Standard*, you're a chump!"

"*You're* the chump!" she snapped. "Wallace isn't against the play! He's helping the play!"

"Wallace is weird," I retorted. I personally had no problem picturing him pretending to work on the play every afternoon, and sneaking into school the next morning to torpedo it. (And it wasn't because he was a complex character. He was just plain rotten.)

But for the good of the drama club, I kept quiet about Wallace. It wasn't easy, but I acted just as thrilled as everybody else to have Laszlo Tamas on a moped. The serious actress in me appreciated that our cast was so pumped up; my common sense told me that our new opening scene was bizarre with a capital B.

But when you've been friends with someone since third grade, it's hard to shake them. So it was automatic for me to plunk my tray down next to Trudi at lunch that day. I was already well established on the bench before I realized who else was sitting at the table. It was my (dis)honor to be dining with Wallace Wallace.

"Oh, it's you," we both chorused. I was still a little embarrassed around him after my meltdown.

"Laszlo's the greatest," raved Trudi, exercising her world-renowned sucking-up muscle. "I'm going to teach him a new cool English word every day. Today's is MTV."

Wallace raised an eyebrow. "What's tomorrow's— HBO?"

So help me, I was just about to say the same thing. But coming from him, it sounded rude and insulting.

"Don't laugh with your mouth full," I mumbled at Trudi, who was yukking it up like a hyena. To her, whatever Wallace said was witty and perfect.

There was a thump as Rory Piper, a pint-sized seventh grader, vaulted the bench, landing expertly in the seat opposite Wallace.

"Nice shot," Wallace commented.

"You should see it on Rollerblades." Rory grinned.

Everything about Rory happened at double-speed; the way he ate, the way he moved, and especially the way he talked. "I hear you guys have got some pretty amazing things happening with the school play."

I was impressed. Usually nobody cared about the drama department. "Well," I began modestly, "we've been working with Mr. Fogelman—"

Rory waved a hand in my face. "Hang on a sec, Rachel, I'm talking to Wallace here." He turned his back on me. "Laszlo says you guys are working up a monster opening to *Old Shep, My Pal*. You think there's a part for me in there?"

"Of course not," I said peevishly. "The play was cast weeks ago."

But Wallace was taking this dumb request seriously. "What did you have in mind?" he asked Rory.

"Rollerblading, man!" cried Rory. "I *rule*! You send me out on the stage to work a little magic. Forget the rest, 'cause I'm the best!"

I must have looked like I was about to choke on my sandwich, because Trudi offered me her water glass. "Listen, Rory," I managed between gulps, "there isn't any Rollerblading in *Old Shep, My Pal*."

"But I'm *awesome*!" he insisted.

Wallace looked thoughtful. "Laszlo's pretty good on the moped, but the scene needs something more. Maybe we should put Rory onstage to chase Old Shep in front of the motorcycle. I've always wondered why that stupid mutt ran out in the middle of the road. It'll make more sense if someone's after him." He frowned. "Who chases a dog?"

"A dogcatcher!" Trudi jumped in.

I thought I was going to die. "*What* dogcatcher?"

"The Rollerblading dogcatcher." Wallace was getting excited. "With Rory doing his thing around the Laments, the moving toy dog, and Laszlo on the moped, it could be pretty spectacular."

"It's perfect," Trudi applauded.

Rory was just as impressed. "Man, I am *in*! I'll see you at rehearsal this afternoon. And Wallace, dude, get ready to be amazed, because I'm bringing my 'blades!"

I chomped down hard on my tongue (ouch). It wasn't my job to tell them that none of this was going to happen. That was why we had a director.

> *. . . Julia, if Brad Pitt was casting a*
> *Rollerblading dogcatcher in your movie,*
> *wouldn't you have to tell the director? I*
> *realize you're probably not a tattletale.*
> *Neither am I. But I had to do something . . .*

When the bell rang at three-thirty, I raced down to Mr. Fogelman's office to talk to him before rehearsal. I was so upset that I just started babbling even before I barged through his half-open door.

"Mr. Fogelman, I don't know how to tell you this—"

I froze. The director was on his hands and knees in the midst of a mountain of crumpled-up paper towels, scrubbing at a stack of colored folders.

He looked up at me. "Somebody poured pancake syrup in my filing cabinet!"

I dropped to my knees, grabbed a towel, and did what I could to help. "Do you think it's another attack on the play?"

"You bet I do," the teacher said in annoyance. "Look at this—the only files that are damaged are the ones on *Old Shep, My Pal.*"

It was a mess. Syrup and paper don't mix. Poor Mr. Fogelman's notes were glued together, and soaked through with the sticky slime. In no time, I was in it up to the elbows, and little bits of paper were starting to stick to me. I'd always loved maple syrup until I saw what it could do to a script. (Yuck!)

"Did he break into your office?" I asked.

"Did who break into my office?"

Who? Everybody knew it was Wallace Wallace. But I said, "You know—the person who did this."

We stared at each other. He didn't speak, and neither did I.

"I keep my door unlocked," he said finally. He added, "But we don't know who did this. Even if we think we do, we don't."

All this talking (or not talking) about Wallace reminded me why I'd come to see our director in the first place.

"Mr. Fogelman, I hate to tell you this, but I've got some more bad news. You'll never believe what's going to happen at rehearsal!"

The Wallace vein in his forehead throbbed as I explained that *Old Shep, My Pal* now starred Rory Piper as the Rollerblading dogcatcher.

"We'll see about this!" he roared, cleaning his sticky hands with a Wet-Nap.

He stormed out into the hall, taking steps so large that I had to jog along beside him. Down the corridor, around the bend, and into the gym he swooped like an avenging angel.

Suddenly, I pulled up short, and beside me, Mr. Fogelman did the same. We stared.

Rory Piper was Rollerblading, and he was amazing

to behold. He streaked across the stage, his feet just a blur, executing jumps and spins and funky dance steps. In his hands he brandished a large butterfly net, which he waved at Old Shep. Yes, the dog was there, too, mounted on a remote-control car, "running" around the road, narrowly avoiding the dogcatcher's swooping net. It was so crazy, and yet it was almost graceful, like a ballet. Rory moved on the Rollerblades as if they were extensions of his feet.

All at once, there was a roar of machinery. From the wings Laszlo Tamas sped onto the scene, mounted on his moped, which had been decorated to look like a Harley. He wore hockey headgear instead of a motorcycle helmet, but you could see the pure concentration through the face guard as he aimed his front tire at Old Shep.

*Thump!*

The stuffed animal went one way, the toy car went another. The bump sent Laszlo's helmet flying. It ricocheted softly off the curtain, and plopped into the butterfly net. Laszlo kept riding straight down the stairs, and came to a screeching halt under the near basketball net.

The cast and crew leaped to their feet in a standing ovation. My confusion almost tore me in two. Yes,

I know, I'd come here to blast this dogcatcher thing out of the water. But a true actress couldn't help but recognize great theater. This was pure entertainment. I looked to Mr. Fogelman for guidance. Surely a real professional writer would know what to do.

Our director's expression was unreadable. Then he began to clap, slowly at first, but with growing enthusiasm.

Everton Wu ran out from the wings, triumphantly waving the remote control for Old Shep. "It was amazing!" he howled.

Instantly, he was set upon by his fellow stagehands with backslaps of congratulations.

Flushed with victory, Rory took a Rollerblading suicide leap off the side of the stage into the arms of a wildly celebrating Laszlo.

Naturally, Trudi was the first person to gush all over Wallace. Right in front of everybody, she threw her arms around his neck and planted a humongous kiss on his smarmy cheek. I was humiliated on her (idiotic) behalf.

My disgust was interrupted by Vito's voice: "Wait a minute! It isn't fair!"

Nathaniel jumped all over this. "Right! Right!" he

cried. "You bet it isn't fair! Vito and I object! Tell them, Vito!"

"How come Rory gets to have all the fun?" Vito demanded. "I want to be on Rollerblades, too."

The color drained out of Nathaniel's face. "What?"

"Yeah!" Trudi shrieked. "All the Lamont kids should be on Rollerblades for the first scene! Wallace, can we do it?"

"We'll try it at tomorrow's rehearsal," Wallace agreed. Then, as an afterthought, he looked at Mr. Fogelman. "Okay?"

"Thank you for asking," the director said with sarcastic politeness. He thought it over. "If you people can Rollerblade around the stage without bumping into one another and breaking your necks, I suppose it's worth a try."

Nathaniel was sputtering with rage and dismay. "But—but—I've never been on Rollerblades!"

"Yo, man, this is your lucky day," Rory assured him. "Because I am a one-man clinic on wheels! Step right up, and I'll have you hot-dogging in no time!"

"But I don't want to hot-dog!" Nathaniel wailed.

*. . . well, what would you do, Julia? If even*
*Mr. Fogelman is willing to go along with*

*this, I have to have faith. Yes, Wallace is
only doing it to mess us up. But the drama
club will have the last laugh. We'll pick his
brains, and use his talent (strange but true;
this football player has talent) to make* Old
Shep, My Pal *the greatest play in the history
of Bedford Middle School.*

   *Keep your fingers crossed for us,*
                                    *Rachel Turner*

# Enter . . .

# MR. FOGELMAN

**MEMO: A director must never lose control of his play.**

I didn't actually see the moment when Wallace officially took over *Old Shep, My Pal.* Oh, it definitely happened. But I must have been in the bathroom, or adjusting a spotlight, or bickering with Wallace over his book review.

It didn't really sink in until that Friday morning. When I passed Trudi Davis in the hall, she called out, "Way to go, Mr. Fogelman! You've done it again!"

In my mind, I went over everything I'd accomplished so far that day. I woke up, had breakfast, walked the dog, drove to school. I stopped and filled the car up with gas, but that hardly seemed worth a "Way to go!"

In my mailbox at the office I found a note on the subject, whatever it was: *Great idea! Can't wait for the next rehearsal!—Everton.*

On the way to third period it happened again. As I fought the usual class-change crowd, Vito was waving and cheering. "You're aces, Mr. Fogelman!"

"Why?" I cried in frustration.

As I stood fuming, Laszlo Tamas walked up and shook my hand.

"Laszlo, wait!" I yelled at his back. "Please tell me what's going on!"

He turned. "You are a wonderful director to have Wallace Wallace on your side."

At that moment, Rachel Turner passed by. She looked at me with such deep pity that I knew. Wallace had come up with another "brilliant" idea for the play. And as usual, I was the last person to know about it.

I thought of the famous Chinese water torture. A prisoner is tied up and blindfolded, and every hour or so, his interrogators allow a single droplet of water to fall on the top of his head. There is no pain, but the victim actually drives himself crazy waiting for the next drip. Well, there was a drip out there with my name on it.

I could only cringe when I imagined what terrible changes might be in store. For all I knew, Wallace had moved the play to prehistoric times. Old Shep was now a saber-toothed tiger who'd been stepped on by a woolly mammoth. It was more than I could bear.

**MEMO: Stay calm.**

"Mr. Fogelman, can I go to the bathroom?"

*"No!"* I bellowed. *"If I can't put on a simple little school play, why should everybody else be able to get on with their lives?"*

My class of quiet sixth graders stared at me, stunned. I apologized and sent them to the library to work on research papers. I moved to the teachers' lounge to calm my nerves by grading essays.

"Problems?" Coach Wrigley sat down on the couch beside me.

"Oh, no," I said quickly. If the people of Bedford knew how much time the coach spent in here drinking coffee, they might blame the Giants' terrible season on something other than the absence of Wallace Wallace. "Why do you ask?"

He pointed to the paper in front of me. "You just

gave some kid an H. Let me guess. Does this have anything to do with a certain football player?"

"I—I need a word with Wallace, yes." And as soon as I said it, I remembered that this was a faculty meeting Friday. Rehearsal was canceled. I'd have to wait three whole days to learn of Wallace's latest "improvement." An entire weekend of Chinese water torture.

The coach read my mind. "Page him out of class. Guidance has all the student schedules. They'll find him for you."

## MEMO: Know how to spot a great idea!

The guidance secretary said Wallace was in math. As I headed for the main office to place the page, three figures blocked the doorway. One was Joey Quick from my seventh-period class. The others were older boys, probably from the high school.

"Hey, Mr. F.," Joey greeted.

"Excuse me, boys," I said, trying to sneak through, "but there's something very important—"

They continued to bar my way. "It's us!" crowed Joey.

I cleared a path with my hands. "You don't understand. This has to do with the play."

"Right!" Joey exclaimed. "We're the Dead Mangoes!"

"The what?" Then I remembered. Joey played lead guitar in his brother Owen's rock band. The kid wrote essay after essay about the hit songs the Dead Mangoes would record, the huge stadium concerts they'd perform, and the millions of dollars they'd earn. The high school boy on the right looked like an older Joey, so I assumed this was Owen.

"Actually," Owen admitted in a deeper version of Joey's voice, "we *were* the Dead Mangoes until our singer quit. So me, Joey, and the Void are looking for our next gig."

"*The Void?*" I regarded the third member of the group, a boy with stringy black bangs that completely covered the top half of his face.

"Our drummer," Joey supplied.

The Void shook his head, and the bangs parted, revealing scornful, beady eyes. "My real name is Myron Muckenfuss," he grunted.

"Last week," Joey enthused, "I took a shortcut through the gym. And I saw something truly cosmic going on there. It was like a Rollerblading, dogcatching, mopeding *party*! And I said to myself, 'Joey, what these guys need is a soundtrack. They need the Dead Mangoes.'"

"Now, Joey," I chuckled, "the production is in two weeks. It's far too late to attempt a major change like—"

"But it's a done deal!" Joey interrupted. "Wallace says the whole cast is totally psyched! We start on Monday!"

It all came crashing down on me. *This* was what all the fuss was about! Wallace was taking my entire play, and setting it to the music of a teenage rock band!

**MEMO: Put your foot down!**
But how could I? If I said no, there'd be another cast revolt, and the play would end up canceled. So when I got rid of Joey and company, I sat down in the faculty room and weighed my options. There was only one course of action.

**MEMO: Do something drastic. And fast.**

# Enter...
# WALLACE WALLACE

**Parker Schmidt's E-News Page**

## Lions 40, Giants 6

Still plagued by the absence of Wallace Wallace,
the Bedford Middle School Giants lost again on
Saturday, dropping their record to 0 and 4.

According to Wallace, still on the inactive
list, this humiliating defeat is the best the team
can do without him . . .

I thought I was going to have a heart attack. What
I'd really said to Parker when he called was "The

Giants always do their best." The guy was a menace!

Ever since Parker made me a secret agent, I'd sworn off the Bedford Middle School *Weekly Standard*. But now that I couldn't go to the games anymore, my only source of news about the Giants was Parker's Web site, which the kids all called porkzit.com. Not that there was much news about the team in his column.

> What's really up with Wallace Wallace? We may never know. But this fourth crushing defeat makes Giants fans wonder if we'll ever again experience the excitement of his heroic leap that brought the county championship to Bedford . . .

What a crock! Funny how Parker remembered my touchdown so well, but the season I spent on the bench never made it into print. No wonder Cavanaugh was in a permanent bad mood. According to the stats, he'd gained ninety yards and kicked two field goals, but Parker never said a word about that. Everyone was fixated on me, the absent benchwarmer-star.

Just then, something whipped by my bedroom window. I rushed over and leaned out. It was Nathaniel Spitzner, rocketing down my street on Rollerblades.

He was flailing his arms in terror, but his legs weren't moving at all. They must have moved at some point, though. Either that or somebody gave him an atomic push, because he was *flying*—and screaming. What was he saying?

"*He-e-e-elp!*"

Rory Piper flashed by in hot pursuit, shouting encouragement. "Bend your knees, dude! Watch out for that tree!"

For me it was the first sign that *Old Shep, My Pal* was getting out of hand. If a stink-bug like Spitzner was learning in-line skating to keep up with the play, that was something Zack Paris himself never would have dreamed of. Then again, Zack Paris was, is, and always will be the world's lousiest writer, so who cares about his boring dreams anyway?

I guess the tree missed Spitzner, because I didn't hear any ambulance sirens or anything like that. What I did hear was a knock on my door. It was probably Rick or Feather, come to moan and groan about the game. I knew it wouldn't be any other Giant, because those guys weren't speaking to me anymore. Kevin wouldn't even look in my direction when I passed him in the hall at school. I was getting kind of sick of staring at the backs of heads. Cavanaugh would talk to me, of course—but only to rub it in that I was Public Enemy Number One.

But it was my mother who poked her head inside. "Wally, telephone. Some boy named Vito. He says it's really urgent."

What was Vito's life-and-death emergency?

"Wallace? Great, you're home. Listen—when Morry Lamont is Rollerblading in Scene One, should I still be playing with the yo-yo? Because I've been working on skating and yo-yoing at the same time. It's a little hard to see where you're going, but the doctor said the swelling should go down by the performance."

Doctor? Swelling? I didn't ask. I just told him to stick to Rollerblading, and he could yo-yo in some other scene.

Amazing! *Old Shep, My Pal*, which had started out as the floor show for my detentions, was creeping into every part of my life. In a weird way, I was even starting to feel I had a stake in it.

That's why I jumped at the chance to have Joey Quick's band provide music for the play. Everybody knew that Joey was the best musician at Bedford Middle School. And the Dead Mangoes played great rock-and-roll—raw-edged, but with a real funky beat.

They were every bit as good as a professional adult band.

I mean, I was no drama freak. But why should the play be lousy when it could be great?

By the time I got to rehearsal on Monday, the Dead Mangoes were best friends with most of the cast. Laszlo had the Void locked in a bear hug. The band's demo tape was playing on Joey's boom box, and there was a lot of clapping and dancing going on.

Mr. Fogelman walked in. "Attention, everybody! I have an important announcement!"

Joey switched off the tape, and we all quieted down.

I was surprised at how calm our director looked. I was expecting a big stink over the Dead Mangoes, a real crab-o-rama, with Spitzner whining backup, and maybe even a little screaming opera from Rachel.

"As you know, the director went on, "Wallace has been with us for well over a month, and even though he still hasn't turned in a review of *Old Shep, My Pal*, he's given us a lot of valuable suggestions. I think we owe him a round of applause."

It was pretty embarrassing. They cheered like I was Michael Jordan. Vito and Rory slapped me on the back. Trudi *kissed* me. But through all the admiration,

I was suspicious. This didn't sound like the Fogelman I knew. What was he up to?

"His help on this play amounts to far more than a simple book review," the director continued. He smiled at me. "And so, Wallace, as of today, your detention is officially over. You can go back to your friends on the Giants."

I snapped to attention in the shocked silence. Over? Go back? I guess I'd been on detention for so long I'd forgotten why I was there.

Unbelievable! I was getting everything I wanted! And how did I feel?

Angry!

That lousy Fogelman wasn't letting *me* off the hook. He was letting *himself* off! He had figured out that the only way to regain control of his crummy play was to get rid of me. Now he could ax the music, water down my changes, and turn *Old Shep, My Pal* into the boring waste of time it was always destined to be.

On the other hand, what did I care? I was free. I was a Giant again. I'd get my friends back, my life back, Cavanaugh would have to shut up, and detention would be nothing more than a rotten memory. I'd still be a benchwarmer, of course. But I was never a star, no matter what Rick said.

I was mobbed by a crowd of well-wishers. I had to duck to avoid Rory's flailing elbows. Laszlo nearly squashed me to death. Vito had tears in his eyes.

"Stop!" I chuckled. "You're crushing me!"

I slapped all their high fives. For some reason I couldn't stop laughing. Partly because it was funny that a detention had made me so loved. But mostly because their good wishes were 100 percent genuine.

Fogelman called everybody away for Scene One. Reluctantly, Trudi, Rory, Laszlo, and Vito left the crowd around me, and climbed up on the stage.

What a great bunch of guys! They were sad to lose me, but happy for me, too. The next time I caught wind of some football player picking on the drama nerds, I'd straighten him out. Unless the nerd happened to be Spitzner. Or Rachel. Man, did she hate me. Too bad. It's tough to find a girl who speaks her mind.

Now the thought of being rid of me put a grin on her mug like she had just won all fifty state lotteries at the same time. She did kind of have a nice smile, though.

I whistled for attention. "This play could be a real winner!" I called. "Two weeks from now I'll be in the front row cheering you guys on!" With a sideways look at Mr. Fogelman, I added, "Don't let anybody make you change the things about it you know are good!"

As I headed out, I remembered that football practice was canceled today. Instead, there was a big Giants pep rally in the cafeteria. I quickened my step. It was the ideal place to make the announcement that I was back.

I heard the funky beat of the Dead Mangoes coming from the boom box. Rehearsal had begun, and the dogcatcher and the Lamonts were on Rollerblades to the tune of Joey Quick's band. I couldn't help noticing how perfectly the music made the action come alive. I felt a surge of satisfaction as I stepped out into the hall.

Screaming voices drew me back inside. Some of the crew were pointing and yelling at a dark wave creeping across the stage from the wings. From my weird angle it looked like army ants, but it was moving too fast. I ran up for a better view, and gawked. Marbles—hundreds of them—were rolling over the stage floor. When they reached the Rollerbladers—

"Watch out!" I shouted, but it was too late.

Vito was the first to fall, then Trudi. Rachel desperately grabbed hold of the curtain cord as her legs slipped out from under her. She went down, pulling the curtain shut, and cutting the rest of us off from the mayhem onstage.

"What's going on?" demanded Mr. Fogelman.

The sound was like machine-gun fire as the marbles rolled off the edge of the stage, and dropped to the hardwood floor of the gym.

Owen Quick stopped the tape. "Man, middle school's *changed*!"

I leaped up to the stage and searched the curtain for the opening, bursting through just in time to see Nathaniel Spitzner take a spill. His pudgy stomach landed on enough marbles to propel him forward along the floor. He rolled right past the main set, off-stage, and straight into Old Shep's doghouse.

That's when it hit me. This wasn't the kind of booby trap you could set up in advance! You'd have to dump those marbles right in the stage entrance. Which meant that the culprit was still around!

I bolted for the door.

"Don't you dare sneak away from this!" Rachel cried.

But I was a man on a mission. I was going to get this guy if I had to tear the school apart brick by brick.

The halls were deserted, and then I caught sight of

the jam-packed cafeteria. The pep rally! Number one Giants fan Dylan Turner was right by the door.

"Hey, Dylan!" I cried. "Did you see anybody coming out of the gym?"

But the runt took one look at me heading in the direction of the rally, and put two and two together. He freaked. *"Hey, look, it's Wallace Wallace! He's back!"*

I scanned the cafeteria. Half the school was there. Worse, all my suspects—the entire Giants team— were at the very front, right by a door that was ten feet from the stage entrance. Any one of them could have dumped the marbles, and waltzed into the rally three seconds later. It was another dead end.

I sighed with resignation. At least it wasn't my problem anymore. I was back on the team.

I savored the cheers as I jogged to the front. I had to squeeze out of this pep rally an entire month of football I'd been robbed of. And when I caught sight of the stricken look on Cavanaugh's face, I really played it up. It was almost like a lie, but I couldn't resist. I did the whole hero gig—throwing my arms up in the air, signaling the V for victory, riling the crowd. And yet—

I wasn't quite as happy as I expected to be. First of

all, I could hear the handful of boos and moosecalls underneath the cheers as I took my place among the other Giants. Second, except for Rick and Feather, my teammates had treated me like garbage this past couple of weeks. Even now, Kevin wore a nasty sneer as I exchanged high fives with some of the players. And as for Cavanaugh, well, with friends like him, who needs Dracula?

Even worse, one of these guys was guilty of the attacks on the play. I mean, talk about poor sportsmanship! The Giants could take a lesson in classiness from the drama nerds. They treated me like gold even when I was walking out the gym door. Now, thanks to me, Fogelman was back in charge, and the play was headed straight down the toilet.

It was too bad, really. The cast and crew deserved a success. They'd earned my loyalty a whole lot more than the Giants had.

Coach Wrigley waved his arms, and the cafeteria quieted down. "Wallace, what a surprise," he greeted me. "Have you come here to tell us something?"

"Yeah, Coach." I faced the crowd. "As of today my detention is officially over—"

A roar of approval rocked the cafeteria. Rick and Feather were slapping each other on the back so hard

I thought they'd need X rays to check for internal injuries.

Finally, the room calmed down, and I went on. "So I'm quitting the team to go back and work on *Old Shep, My Pal.*"

*What?!* Did *I* say that?

An enormous gasp sucked all the air out of the cafeteria. For an instant, I was at the center of attention, surrounded by total silence. But I was the most shocked guy in the place. If somebody had told me I was going to do that, I would have bet him a million dollars he was crazy. It definitely wasn't my brain talking. Those words had come straight from my gut.

One thing decided it for me. Wallace Wallace never lied. I said it so I must have meant it. "That's all," I finished, and headed for the door.

As I marched out, I heard Rick Falconi behind me. "I'm hitting the fan! I'm totally hitting the fan!"

They caught up with me about halfway home—Rick and Feather, I mean.

If Rick had hit the fan back in the cafeteria, by now he was going through the jet engine of a 747. "Are you *crazy*, Wallace?" he howled, his face purple.

Feather was a little more in control, but you could

see he was pretty upset. "I don't get it," he told me. "I thought you wanted this. I thought you *liked* being on the team."

"It's nothing against you," I said honestly, "but most of the Giants haven't been the best of friends lately."

"Who listens to Cavanaugh?" Rick moaned.

"It's not just Cavanaugh," I insisted. "But these drama people really stood by me, even when it looked like I was trying to mess up their play."

"But it's only a *play*!" Feather wailed. "A bunch of guys in goofy costumes saying fake things! How can you compare that to football?"

"I can't," I admitted. "A play is completely different. But it's just as good in its own way."

"It's not fair," Feather complained. "I ate all that celery for nothing!"

"This is a joke, right?" Rick pleaded. "A really cruel, sick, unfunny joke?"

"I'm sorry," I said, hating to hurt my two closest friends. "But I'm not coming back to the team."

Rick turned very white, then very red. "I am never going to forgive you, man! This is the *end* between you and me! I refuse to be friends with a Benedict Omelette like you!"

Feather pulled a Ziploc bag from his pocket, ripped it open dramatically, and dumped out three stalks of celery. With the heel of his sneaker, he ground them into the dirt.

The two of them stormed away.

I felt like Benedict Omelette.

# Enter...

# TRUDI DAVIS

**I CAN'T BELIEVE** I ever thought Mrs. Mcconville was cool.

She was, like, so 1990s! When I suggested the library should cancel its subscription to *Teen Dazzle* magazine and switch to *Cosmo*, she got all bent out of shape.

"But you love *Teen Dazzle!*"

"It's so juvenile," I complained. "Who cares about friendship rings and glitter makeup? I need hardcore advice on my love life."

She got really pale. "Love life?"

"That's just it! I don't have one. And I *need* one.

That's where *Cosmo* comes in. They've got an article called 'Get Your Man to Notice You.' I'd buy it myself, but I'm broke. I've decided to go auburn, and Rascal Red is the most expensive hair color on the market."

Rascal Red! What a scam that turned out to be! When I got out of the shower and showed Rachel, she said, "You look like somebody dumped a pot of chili on your head."

I looked in the mirror. She was right! This was getting totally serious. It would take weeks for the stuff to wash out! By then, Wallace Wallace could have another girlfriend.

I tried everything. New jeans; a frosted lipstick; heels so high Coach Wrigley recruited me for girls' basketball; sexy perfume. Nada. Wallace didn't notice a thing, except maybe the perfume—he was allergic to it. No refunds, either, especially when the bottle is half empty.

It was frustrating in the extreme. Now that the word was out that Wallace had quit the Giants to work on *Old Shep, My Pal*, the whole school was, like, suddenly interested in our play. There were so many kids nosing around that Mr. Fogelman had to close the rehearsals to spectators. So every day, there

I was, locked in the gym with Wallace for a whole hour, and I still couldn't attract his attention! Not even with my clip-on belly-button ring. How pathetic is that?

The cast and crew banded together and agreed that we wouldn't talk about the play outside of rehearsals.

"And whatever you do," added Wallace, "don't say anything to Porker Zit. By the time he gets through with it, *Old Shep, My Pal* will be an underwater Norwegian ballet, starring Navy frogmen and tap-dancing eels."

Wasn't he adorable? What a sense of humor! And smart, too. Sure enough, Parker bounced from cast member to cast member, trying to wheedle an interview. We froze him out. Even me, and you know how I love to talk—especially when I've got some inside info.

There was only one teeny little slipup, but I'm pretty positive I got away with it. I sure hope what happened afterward wasn't my fault.

Here's how it went down: Parker spotted Wallace helping the Dead Mangoes carry some amplifiers into the gym. He cornered me in the parking lot.

"It's a musical, right? And Wallace Wallace is a singer?"

I laughed. "Don't be stupid. My sweetie couldn't even carry a tune."

He stiffened like a pointer. "*Sweetie?* Are you Wallace's girlfriend?"

Well, who could blame me? I was getting nowhere with Wallace, and this was my chance to be his girlfriend, even if it was only for the, like, half a second it would take to say yes.

So I said it.

Was that so terrible?

# Loverboy Football Hero Follows His Heart, Quits Team to Join Girlfriend in *Old Shep, My Pal*

by Parker Schmidt, Staff Reporter

He did it all for love.

This reporter has finally discovered the truth behind Wallace Wallace's absence from the Giants. The gridiron superstar has been carrying on a secret romance with seventh-grade actress Trudi Davis, who will be appearing as Tori Lamont in the upcoming drama club production of *Old Shep, My Pal.*

Miss Davis didn't say whether she would be working with Wallace to pull his English grade up from an incomplete. . . .

# Enter . . .
# **RACHEL TURNER**

*Dear Julia,*

*Now I know what it feels like to go crazy. Everything you thought you knew gets turned inside out and backward. Gravity pulls up; the sun is dark; fish swim through the air; chocolate is low-cal; and Wallace Wallace quits the football team to devote his life to* Old Shep, My Pal.

*And then—THEN—you open your school newspaper . . .*

"Honest, Rachel, it isn't my fault!" Trudi defended

herself on the phone. "Parker's psycho! He made it all up! I had nothing to do with it!"

"Oh, sure!" I was so mad, I almost chewed the receiver. "Every time Wallace sticks out his foot, you're beating off the competition to be the first to fall to your knees and kiss it. I know you, Trudi. You love these rumors, even if you have to spread them yourself."

"Parker blew everything out of proportion!" she insisted. "I never said that stuff about how Wallace's loneliness during football practice was eating him up inside—although it *is* a very sweet thought—"

"I'm not the one you have to explain it to," I told her. "Your so-called *sweetie* must be ready to kill you by now."

"I've already called Wallace and straightened out the whole wacky business."

"And he wasn't mad?" That didn't sound like the kind and understanding (not) Wallace that I knew.

"Well, actually, he wasn't home," Trudi confessed. "But I explained everything on his answering machine."

"He's probably burning the tape right now—" I began.

*Crash!*

I lifted the blinds. A stream of garbage was sailing down into the yard from the window next to mine.

"Trudi, I'll call you back!" I slammed down the receiver and shouted, "Dylan, what are you doing?"

He didn't answer. He just kept hurling stuff.

I burst in the door of Dylan's Chamber of Horrors. Through the hanging spider webs and mummy bandages I could see the pile of stuff by the window, waiting to be flung. It was all his lovingly collected football memorabilia—his framed pictures and mementos of Wallace's big touchdown, his Giants helmet and jersey, his pennants, T-shirts, his miniature of the county championship trophy, and even his dried-up square of turf from the end zone where the Giants won it all last year.

"Dylan, don't!" I pleaded. "You love this stuff!"

"Get out of here, Rachel!" he warned. "I don't want anything to do with you! You're part of the play that brainwashed Wallace Wallace!"

I rushed over and slammed his window shut. "To be brainwashed, first you have to have a brain!"

But he was really upset. "It's not funny! At least when he was on detention, he had no choice! Now he doesn't even *want* to be a Giant, thanks to your rotten stinking play and your rotten stinking friend!"

"You think *I'm* thrilled about it?" I countered. "I was so happy when I thought we were rid of that jock! Now we're stuck with him forever! So if you want to feel sorry for somebody, try *me*!"

In a way, it was the closest I'd ever been with my little brother. It tore him up that Wallace was off football and on drama, and I was just as upset about exactly the same thing.

The next morning when we got to school, I wasn't surprised to find that someone had written *FEMME FATALE* on Trudi's locker in Magic Marker. The part that blew me away was that Wallace Wallace was there, armed with a bucket and sponge, scrubbing it off.

He looked at Trudi, and I stepped protectively between them. "Don't you dare yell at her!"

He shrugged as he looked at us. "Sorry. My fault."

I was bug-eyed. Of all the things I'd expected, this was dead last on the list. *"Your* fault?"

He shifted uncomfortably and continued to address Trudi. "It's Porker Zit. The guy's got it in for me, for some reason. And you got caught in the crossfire."

"Oh, hey, no problem," Trudi said graciously. "Sticks and stones, right?"

He finished the cleanup, mumbled, "See you guys at rehearsal," and rushed away.

Trudi turned to me. "There's something totally, like, deep between me and Wallace," she insisted.

I rolled my eyes. "Yeah? What?"

"Well, if you could just say it, it wouldn't be deep, would it?"

(Sheesh!)

Hanging out with Trudi that day was like accompanying a movie star on a stroll through Beverly Hills. Kids in the hall stopped and stared at her. Pointing fingers followed us like compass needles. Whispered conversations swirled around us as we passed by.

"That's her! That's Wallace's girlfriend."

"Girlfriend? She's his fiancée."

"He gave up football for her!"

One fifth grader exclaimed to his friend, "Hey, look! That's Wallace Wallace's leading lady!"

I grabbed the poor kid by his collar, and shouted right into his face, "Wallace Wallace isn't an actor! He isn't even *in* the play! But if he was, his leading lady wouldn't be *her*! It would be *me*!"

Trudi looked at me with such shock that I got all flustered. "Well, my part is bigger than yours, and I'm going to be a real actress one day, and why does everybody think Wallace is the toast of Broadway just because he used to wear cleats?"

"Calm down," Trudi soothed. "You can't blame people for being interested. The greatest Giant ever just threw it all away; rehearsals are locked up tight; loud music is blasting from the gym—we're the hottest ticket at school!"

I snorted. "You're loving this, aren't you?"

She threw her arms wide. "What's not to love? Before all this, we were a couple of nothing seventh graders. Now we're in on the biggest thing since Wallace's touchdown. Eighth graders talk to us! Do you realize that if Wallace had a party tonight, we'd probably be invited?"

I made a face. "If Wallace invited me to his house to pick up my ten-million-dollar check from Publishers Clearing House, I wouldn't go."

Trudi looked impatient. "You're the one who always complains that nobody cares about the drama club. Well, now *everybody* cares. And our play is shaping up into a monster hit! Life is good, Rachel! Enjoy it!"

*. . . Do you think she could be right, Julia?*
*Are my dreams really coming true, but I'm*

*too uptight to appreciate it? And if so, what's
wrong with me?*

*Remember we made up an example about
you shooting a movie with Brad Pitt? What
if, in spite of everything, the movie turned
out to win Best Picture of the Year? Would
you still be so mad at Brad Pitt that you
couldn't enjoy your success?*

*You must think I'm awfully selfish,
worrying about me, me, me all the time.
But the person I really feel sorry for is our
director. The shock of having gotten rid
of Wallace only to have him bounce back
the very next day must have broken his
spirit. He barely puts up a fuss while Wallace
runs the whole show. Really, Julia, can you
blame him? If he tried to bring us back to his
original script (or even halfway) the whole
cast would quit. There would just be Mr.
Fogelman, me, and a kid named Nathaniel
Spitzner. That wouldn't sell too many tickets
for opening night . . .*

When I heard that Wallace was changing the role of
the vet, by turning all her dialogue into rap, I rushed

right over to Mr. Fogelman's office to offer some sympathy and moral support.

My head was spinning as I walked. Now, instead of "Your beloved pet has expired," Leticia's lines went more like:

"Go shop for a canary, or a turtle, or a frog.
'Cause you no longer own a dog."

I suppose that was a jock's idea of poignant and beautiful.

I tapped on the door of the teacher's office, and walked in. "Mr. Fogelman, I'm so sor—" The astonishing sight and sound within that room stopped me dead in my tracks.

The three Dead Mangoes were draped in various poses around the cramped quarters. The Quick brothers were strumming madly on their unplugged guitars. That awful Void person slouched all over the desk, drumming on the blotter, and using the IN/OUT tray as cymbals. Most amazing of all, Mr. Fogelman was perched on an overturned wastebasket. All his concentration was aimed at the small electric keyboard that rested on his knees. They were *jamming*!

And it was great! The best thing about it was Mr.

Fogelman. The Wallace vein was nowhere to be seen as his fingers danced over the keys. He looked as young and carefree as Joey. With a sweep of his hand, he brought their song to a close.

I clapped as loud as I could. "That was fantastic, Mr. Fogelman! I didn't know you could play!"

He seemed kind of embarrassed to be caught in the act. "Oh, you know, I was in a band in college. I'm not very good anymore."

"Are you kidding?" crowed Joey, punctuating it with a power chord. "You're *awesome*! You're going to be the ultimate Dead Mango!"

Mr. Fogelman laughed gently. "Thanks for that, Joe, but I'm not really free to join your band. In case you haven't noticed, I have a job."

"No, he means for the *play*!" Owen explained. "We need your keyboard to get a really big sound for *Old Shep, My Pal*."

"That would be fun," Mr. Fogelman admitted, "but it's impossible. I'm the director."

The Void raised both hands to part the curtain of hair away from his eyes. "*You're* the director?" he frowned. "I thought that guy Wallace was the director."

"No," I said sarcastically. "He's in charge of everything else in the world."

Mr. Fogelman laughed. And I thought to myself, if the Dead Mangoes could put our director in a good mood (even when the W word was mentioned) then they were well worth having in the play.

"Come on, Mr. Fogelman," Joey pleaded. "Without you we're just fantastic. *With* you, we'd be, like, out of control, ballistic, steamroller, wow!"

Suddenly, I blurted, "You should do it, Mr. Fogelman! Wal—*other people* can look after staging and cues." (I'd almost said . . . well, you know.)

I could practically see our director's brain working as he talked himself into it. Finally, he sighed. "The play has changed so much; I guess it can change a little more. Boys, you've got yourself another Mango."

The Bedford fall fair was that weekend. Trudi and I had been going as long as we'd been friends. Yeah, sure, we were getting a little old for the games and the rides. But it was still fun, with the best junk food on earth. My favorite part was the show tent, which really appealed to the actress in me.

"Let's go early like last year," I urged as we walked to homeroom.

"Go where?" asked Trudi airily.

(Earth to Trudi . . .) "Hello! The fair is Saturday."

"The fair?" she repeated. "We've got no time for that. Wallace is raking leaves on Saturday!"

I stared at her. "And I should care about this because . . . ?" I prompted.

"We can't let him do all that work by himself," Trudi reasoned. "It's a big yard. And his dad doesn't live with them, you know."

"You don't live with them either," I reminded her.

I didn't care that my dizzy friend was starting to believe Parker Schmidt's article. Anybody with eyes could see how she laughed at Wallace's jokes, hung around his locker, and even invited him to a cast party at her house (one guest: him. He stayed about forty-five seconds). No, what bothered me was that she was blowing me off, breaking our tradition, to do some jock's yard work!

All day I simmered just below boiling. I looked longingly at the posters advertising this year's fair as the biggest we'd ever had. I must have overheard twenty people from our play alone making plans to meet bright and early Saturday morning:

"Be at my house by eight-thirty. My mom's giving us a lift."

"We'll meet at the Main Street bus."

"Don't be late. There's so much to do."

I thought it over. Why should I miss the fair because Trudi had gone crazy? I had other friends at this school.

I approached Leticia. "Hey, is it all right if I tag along with you guys on Saturday?"

"Sure!" she exclaimed with enthusiasm. "The more the merrier. Don't forget to bring your rake."

My *rake*?!

# Enter . . .
# WALLACE WALLACE

*I* **WAS A GIANT** *again, in my usual spot on the bench. The halftime show was going on in the middle of the game. It was* Old Shep, My Pal, *starring Nathaniel Spitzner on Rollerblades, with musical guests Mr. Fogelman and the Dead Mangoes.*

*Rick took the snap, and whipped the ball over to Laszlo, who took off on his moped, mud kicking up behind the spinning wheels. But Everton Wu was a wizard with his remote control, and the stuffed dog made a beautiful tackle.*

*I was about to jump on the fumble when marbles and pepper and pancake syrup started raining down on the field. It was another attack on the play! My loyal wife Trudi had the culprit in a headlock. He wore a Giants' uniform with a question mark where the number should be. His face was hidden by a cheerleader's megaphone.*

"Wallace!"

*I knew that voice! Was it Rick? Feather? Kevin? Cavanaugh?*

*I pushed away the megaphone to reveal the face of . . .*

"Wally!"

My mother was calling me from downstairs.

"I couldn't see who it was!" I roared out loud.

"Wally, come down. Your friends are here."

I sat up in bed. "Rick?" I asked hopefully. "Feather?" I couldn't believe those guys were talking to me again after I'd quit the team.

I ripped open the curtains to see whose bike was here. I gawked.

It wasn't Rick or Feather, but it seemed like everybody else I knew. Most of the cast and crew of *Old Shep, My Pal* was swarming over my yard, raking.

Laszlo stood guard over an enormous pile of leaves. Vito held open green garbage bags while Rory and Leticia were in charge of stuffing. They were so organized down there that they even had a twist-tie specialist, Everton, who was also responsible for piling the full bundles by the curb. It was like the Giants times a hundred. But I'd always *invited* the team. I hadn't invited anybody for today.

I threw on some clothes, and raced downstairs. It was really nice of everyone, but I was mortified. I mean, the job was half done before I even opened my eyes to start the day.

Trudi was there to greet me as I burst out the side door. "Hi, Wallace! Guess what we're doing!"

Like I wouldn't notice forty people slaving on my lawn. "But why are you here? How did everybody know I was raking today?"

She looked mystified. "You told me."

"*I* told you?" But then I remembered. Ever since that moron Parker Schmidt reported that Trudi was the love of my life, she'd been trying to bamboozle me into acting like it was true. When she hit me up to take her to the fall fair, I was stuck. I couldn't lie, so I made up my mind to rake leaves, and used it as an excuse.

My mother sidled over. "Thanks a lot, Wally, for letting me know you were expecting company."

"I didn't know anybody was coming!" I whispered. "I'm as surprised as you are!"

She pushed a pitcher and a stack of paper cups into my hands. "See that everyone gets juice. I'll go in and throw together a few thousand sandwiches." The look she left me with pretty plainly said that for what this was going to cost us in food, we could have hired Lorenzo of Beverly Hills, Leaf-Raker to the Stars.

Feeling stupid and more than a little ashamed, I became the drink guy. These drama nerds—my *fellow* drama nerds; I was one of them now—they acted like I was doing them a favor by allowing them to work their fingers to the bone in my yard.

"It's the least we can do to thank you for making our play so fantastic," Vito said emotionally.

I have to admit that it felt good to be appreciated. The appreciation level from my former teammates on the Giants had dropped to zero. I glanced around the yard at my rakers and baggers. I definitely wasn't friendless. I'd just made the switch to a different type of friend. While the Giants had all been pretty much the same type of personality, the drama club provided an unbelievable variety. Just in my backyard, I had a piece of work like the Void raking shoulder to shoulder with happy-go-lucky fifth grader Everton Wu. Or a hot dog like Rory working alongside a serious, straitlaced girl like Rachel.

Rachel? I did a double take. It was Rachel, all right.

She hated my guts. Why would she come over to do my yard work?

I went up and offered her a glass of apple juice.

"Thanks." She sniffed the glass like she was checking for poison, then drank thirstily.

"I sort of wouldn't expect you to—you know—be here," I commented, pouring her a refill.

"I'm president of the drama club," she replied evenly. "Where they go, I go." Her expression clearly said she would rather be having her teeth drilled.

I resisted an impulse to empty the pitcher over her head. Why did this girl have such a knack for pushing my buttons? "I was the most surprised guy in the world when I looked out the window this morning," I defended myself. "I didn't ask anybody to come."

I started to walk away. I don't know what made me turn again and say, "Well, anyway, thanks for helping."

She looked kind of surprised. "You're welcome."

Good old Mom. She could always be counted on to roll with the punches. Just as the last leaf was getting bagged, she turned up with two giant platters of sandwiches.

It was perfect timing. The cast and crew of *Old Shep, My Pal* fell on the snack like starving sharks.

I perched on the edge of the picnic table, munching and kind of enjoying this unexpected feast. It was almost a party. Seated on the grass, the rakers were so focused on their food that all I could see was the tops of their heads. I recognized Trudi's reddish mop, mostly by the bouncing that indicated that she was talking nonstop. Beside her, Rachel, dark and wavy, and then Vito's unruly black curls, a sharp contrast to the cascading blond hair next to him.

I stared. Ridiculously straight and shiny—oh, no! It was Bedford's most famous good hair day! What was Cavanaugh doing in *my* yard, eating *my* food, talking to *my* guests?

I marched over to my ex–best friend, grabbed a fistful of that good hair day, and pulled until the jerk was standing beside me.

"I was invited," Cavanaugh beamed, freeing his hair from my grip. It floated down and settled around his head in perfect order. "Your mom said, 'Are you hungry, Stevie?' And you'd have been proud of me, Stupid Stupid. I was honest, just like you. I said yes."

I glowered at him. "You've got no business busting in here on me and my friends—"

*"Friends?!"* He started laughing so hard that he began to choke on his sandwich. I pounded him on the

back because I didn't want him to drop dead—at least, not on my picnic table.

"What a difference a year makes!" Cavanaugh snorted, catching his breath. "Last fall you were the hero, king of Bedford. Now you're clown prince of the geeks."

I saw red. "Listen, Steve—" Yes, I broke my own rule and admitted that this bum had a first name. "These guys have more character in their little fingers than all you Giants will ever have in your whole bodies! They know what it is to work hard on something that nobody cheers for, or thinks it's cool to be part of. There are no trophies for what they do, but they do it anyway, and they give it all they've got! If the football team put in one-sixteenth the effort the drama club is putting into *Old Shep, My Pal*, then maybe you wouldn't be in last place!"

You'd have to really know my ex–best friend to notice the millionth of a second when his perma-grin wavered. What everybody else saw was this friendly football player finishing his sandwich, giving me a familiar pat on the shoulder, and then heading home to get ready for the game that afternoon.

Rachel was looking at me in wide-eyed shock, which meant she was the only one who had overheard my blowup. I'm sure it confirmed what she already thought about me—that I was a bigmouthed jerk.

On Monday at lunch, I tapped lightly on the door of the athletic office in the gym. "Coach? Got a minute?"

Coach Wrigley was at his desk, remote control in hand. "Hi, Wallace. Come on in. Remember this?" He pointed to the screen.

I looked. It was the videotape of our locker room after the championship game last year. There I was with the rest of the guys, jumping up and down, pouring Gatorade all over ourselves. It was bedlam in there—us, the coaches, our parents, and all the fans who could cram themselves in the door.

After everything that had happened this year, it made me really uncomfortable. "How come you're watching this, Coach?"

He laughed without humor. "I'm sure not going to get to tape a celebration like this anytime soon."

"That's kind of what I need to talk about," I admitted. "The guys all hate me. I'm almost getting used to that. I wanted to know if you hate me, too."

He paused the tape, and I couldn't help noticing Cavanaugh in the background, looking pretty sulky amid all that joy. Even the championship was a disappointment if he couldn't be the hero. I was probably witnessing, frozen on the screen, the very instant that he had become my ex–best friend.

"Hate you?" The coach turned in his chair to face me. "Don't be stupid. Why would I hate you?"

"For not writing that book review to get back on the team. And then for quitting."

He heaved a heavy sigh. "Look, kid, I won't pretend that I wouldn't rather have you on the Giants."

I frowned. "I couldn't make the difference between winning and losing."

"We lost by forty-seven points last weekend," Coach Wrigley said grimly. "Jerry Rice couldn't make the difference." He smiled. "No, you don't have great football skills. But there's something about you, Wallace—maybe that famous honesty. It brings out the best in people. I wouldn't be surprised if you're having that effect on the people in the drama club. When the tickets go on sale for *Old Shep, My Pal*, I'll be the first one in line."

I grinned. "It may not be good, but I can guarantee that it won't be boring."

He looked past me, and I realized there was someone standing behind me in the doorway.

"Coach?" I heard Rick's voice. "If you happen to

see Wallace, could you give him—" I turned around, and he fell silent.

"Give me what?" I asked.

In reply, he dropped a large carton at my feet. "I'm not talking to you," he said stiffly. "I'm not even talking to you enough to tell you I'm not talking to you."

"Lighten up, Falconi," groaned the coach.

I looked in the box. It contained everything I'd ever given or loaned Rick—every sweatshirt, baseball cap, CD, even the twenty-three back issues of *Sports Illustrated* from the subscription I'd bought him for his thirteenth birthday.

I picked up the last item in the box, a football. "This isn't mine," I commented.

"Tell Wallace that's the game ball from last Saturday," Rick said to Coach Wrigley. "The other team didn't want it. They said playing us was like beating up on a kindergarten class. And since it's *all his fault*, we voted to give it to him."

The coach snatched the ball away from me. "I'm going to keep this ball right here in the office as a reminder of the 2000 team—not the only Giants who ever lost, but the only ones who tried to blame their troubles on anybody but themselves!"

Rick glared at me. "I'm being nice compared to the rest of the team! They think you're a rat-fink! And all because of some seventh-grade *girl*!"

"It's not true," I defended myself lamely.

"Cavanaugh was right!" Rick blasted me. "All that honesty stuff was a load of hooey! The guys are ready to kill you, man! You should have seen Feather when he saw the *Standard*! He was red as a cucumber!"

Somehow I didn't feel like laughing.

# Enter...
# MR. FOGELMAN

**MEMO: Don't forget to tell Jane about the Dead Mangoes.**

"*Aaaaaaah!*"

As I was plugging in my electric keyboard, I heard my wife scream.

I ran to the front hall. "What is it? What's wrong?"

Jane was cowering behind the ficus tree. "There's a burglar outside!"

I was shocked. "Where?"

Gingerly, she eased aside the curtain in the narrow window beside the door. There on our front step stood a tall, skinny, black-jacketed teenager with his hair hanging in his face.

"Oh," I laughed. "That's not a burglar. That's the Void!"

She was amazed. "You're *expecting* this person?"

"His real name is Myron," I explained. "But he hates it when you call him that." I threw open the door and ushered the boy inside. "We have a doorbell," I informed him. "It makes it easier for us to know you're there."

The Void shook his head until his beady eyes peeked out at us. "Owen and Joey said meet *at* your house, not *in* it."

"Owen and Joey?" Jane turned to face me. "Exactly how many teenagers are coming here tonight?"

Before I could answer, an ancient, rusty van screeched into the driveway, horn blasting. Out jumped the Quick brothers.

"Hey, Mr. F.!" called Owen. "Ready for rehearsal?"

This wasn't exactly how I'd planned to break the news to Jane.

**MEMO: Better late than never.**

"I joined a band," I confessed. "I'm a Mango."

She goggled. "A *what*?"

"A Mango."

"*Dead* Mango," the Void amended.

Joey looked around. "Cool house," he commented. "Kind of clean-air, suburbia, seventies, Brady Bunch, home sweet home."

Jane glared at me. "Well, I'll leave you *children* alone to have your fun. Don't be too loud. You know how Mrs. Vendome complains."

"Oh, no problem," I called. "We're just trying to put together a few songs for *Old Shep, My Pal.* We won't be using amplifiers."

"Uh-huh." She sounded disgusted as she disappeared up the stairs.

"Ooh, Mr. F., that doesn't sound good," Joey whispered. "You could take a lesson from Wallace when it comes to dealing with women. Trudi treats him with *respect.*"

I smiled instead of taking it personally. It was all in response to my latest memo.

**MEMO: Mellow out.**

So I was mellowing. I think it was having a positive effect on me. One afternoon Trudi Davis looked at me in shock and blurted, "You're young!"

I laughed. "I'm twenty-nine. How old did you think I was?"

She shrugged. "I always thought you were, like,

fifty or something. Frowning gives you wrinkles. And those *suits* you wore. No offense, but the dodo is extinct, and so are your ties."

Dressing more casually was something I started when I joined the band. But I felt so much more comfortable that I decided to include it under "mellow out."

Even around Wallace Wallace, I vowed to stay mellow if it killed me. And I found that he wasn't such a rotten kid after all.

Wallace taught me a lesson: if you force the students to fit into the play, it'll come out lifeless and boring. But if you mold the *play* to showcase the talents of the *students*, the sky's the limit.

True, our play was going to be a little out of the ordinary, but it was worth it. I'd never seen kids work so hard.

That's not to say we didn't have problems: rain through a busted skylight warped our set of the Lamont home into a canoe; five days before the performance, Old Shep's remote-control car died mysteriously; in the middle of everything, Leo and his family up and moved to California, so I had to recruit a new Mr. Lamont.

The list was endless—burnt-out spotlights, a wasp

infestation, a twenty-four-hour flu, a locker room toilet that flooded out the gym floor.

"Football players have it easy by comparison" was Wallace's comment. "To be a drama nerd, you have to be a wizard, too!"

"Also a carpenter," I put in. "And a plumber, an exterminator, and an electrician."

"*And* a doctor!" Rachel came racing over. "Leticia's throwing up in the change room."

I didn't panic. Panicking wasn't mellow. And anyway, the problems seemed to bring out the best in those kids.

**MEMO: When things start falling into place, get out of the way; it's a happy avalanche.**

Kelly Ramone and the set designers figured out a way to make it look like it was raining onstage for the thunderstorm in scene four. They lowered strands of Christmas tinsel from the curtain tracks while our lighting people bathed everything in blue. The effect was remarkable.

Wallace recruited the Old Shep Dancers, last-minute volunteers from Mrs. Vasquez's eighth-grade advanced movement class, to add to our musical numbers. Owen and the Void wired extra speakers into the sound system so our live performance would be coming at the audience from all directions. The rebuilt Lamont house turned out to be a masterpiece, with a real working door, and even a little dog door for the title character of our play.

**MEMO: Update Dr. Chechik on recent changes.** I wasn't bragging; I was *warning* the poor man. He might not be as mellow as I was. With rehearsals closed, no one had the slightest idea what we were up to in the gym. Crazy rumors about us buzzed all over the school, and even in the faculty lounge.

I thought back to the time my play opened in New York. There were cast parties and press conferences and hoopla, but still I never felt *this* special.

*The Bedfoard Middle School Drama Club*
*invites you to a musical production of*
### OLD SHEP, MY PAL
*loosely based on the enduring classic novel*
*by Zack Paris*
*Directed by Wallace Wallace and Mr. Fogelman*
*featuring the music of*
*The Dead Mangoes Plus One*
*Saturday, November 21, 8:00 p.m.*
*Tickets: SOLD OUT*

"Sold out?!" I repeated. "How can it be sold out? We haven't even printed the tickets yet!"

"Oh, that was my idea," Trudi confided. "When people hear 'sold out,' they beg to come."

"Well, change it back to five dollars each," Rachel ordered. "Some people might get the crazy idea that sold out means sold out. It wouldn't be much fun without an audience."

"How about 'Good Seats Going Fast'?" Trudi wheedled.

"That's just plain dumb."

I sighed. "Take it easy, people. We're a week away. The only thing that can sink us is ourselves. We have to stay mellow."

**MEMO: Follow your own advice.**

# Enter ...
# RACHEL TURNER

*Dear Julia,*

 *Hi, it's Rachel again. But not the same
Rachel. I've decided to put aside all my bad
feelings and let myself enjoy the upcoming
production, which is turning out fantastic . . .*

I ran straight to the gym first thing Tuesday morning.
Mr. Fogelman and the Dead Mangoes had finished
their final song, "Farewell, Old Pal," and had promised to perform it for us before school. Also, the director had printed brand-new, updated scripts. With the
performance coming up on Saturday, I knew my lines

(and everybody else's). But some of the actors were getting a little confused by the dozens of changes and inserts scribbled on the old copies.

I wanted my new draft, too, but for a different reason. The new script would make the ultimate souvenir. I was positive that Saturday would be the first day of my real acting career.

There was a ruckus going on in the gym when I got there. Everybody was standing on the stage, knee-deep in what looked like snow. Upon closer inspection, I could see that the white piles were made up of tens of thousands of long, thin strips of paper—barely a quarter inch across.

"What is it?" I asked in bewilderment.

Mr. Fogelman supplied the answer, and his face was pure anguish. "Our scripts! Forty-five copies!"

I was astonished. "What happened to them?"

As if on cue, the P.A. system burst into life. *"Would the custodian please come to the office. The paper shredder is missing."*

I felt my blood turn to ice water in my veins. Another attack on the play! Just when it looked like all that was behind us! And only four days to opening night!

That was the very moment that Laszlo, wading

through the piles, stubbed his toe on something hard. He cursed out a long sentence in Hungarian, dug in, and came up with (you guessed it) a paper shredder.

"I can't believe it!" raged Mr. Fogelman. "I spent all weekend at the photocopier! I was collating last night until three o'clock in the morning!"

"There's something else," said Laszlo, foraging around the paper drifts. "Got it!" He pulled the object up, and held it for all to see.

It was a Giants football jersey, the kind the team wore in practice. The front read PROPERTY OF BEDFORD MIDDLE SCHOOL ATHLETICS; the back said one word: WALLACE.

Oh, wow.

I'd heard silence before, but nothing like this. It was so quiet that the footsteps approaching across the wood floor resounded like gunshots.

"Hey, everybody!" exclaimed Wallace. "What's all that stuff?"

"Wallace," breathed Vito, shaking his head. "It was *you*. Right from the very beginning."

"What are you talking about?" asked Wallace. "What are you doing with my old scrimmage shirt?"

"I think," Mr. Fogelman began evenly, "that shredding forty-five scripts is sweaty work. So you took off your jersey and forgot it under all that paper."

"Wait a minute." Wallace took a step backward. "You think *I* did this?"

"The shirt proves it!" Leticia managed tearfully.

"I haven't seen that shirt all year!" Wallace protested.

I was in shock. It was like I wasn't part of this, but I was watching it on TV. I waited for someone to stand up and take Wallace's side. Surely one of these Wallace fans would defend him. Surely *Trudi* would!

I looked at my longtime friend and saw she had tears in her eyes. "Oh, Wallace!" she quavered. "We trusted you! We followed you! We liked you *so much*! And it was you the whole time!"

Wallace looked shocked. "The whole time? You mean you think I did all that other stuff, too?"

"I was just starting to believe in you!" exclaimed Nathaniel.

"This is *awful*!" moaned Joey. "Man, it's like, homework, allergy shot, dentist, bummer!"

Wallace was very white and still. "I thought you guys were my friends."

"We thought you were ours," Trudi barely whispered.

Mr. Fogelman stepped forward, and half a pound

of shredded paper spilled off the stage. Our director was even paler than Wallace. "I don't want to believe this," he said sorrowfully, "but the evidence is right in front of me. Wallace, we can't thank you enough for what you've done for our play. But this is the strangest situation I've ever run into. The kind of person who could build with one hand while tearing down with the other needs to take a long hard look at himself."

That's when I caught a glimpse of the *old* Wallace Wallace, the ramrod-straight back, the stubborn outthrust jaw, the steely resentful expression. "I see myself just fine, Mr. Fogelman."

"Then we don't agree," the director stated gravely. "As of this minute, Wallace, you're banned from all rehearsals. And I don't want to see you at the performance."

Instead of the gasp of horror that I expected, there was a huge, melancholy sigh. It sounded like the wind moaning through the trees outside a haunted house.

Wallace started for the door. Then, almost there, he turned back to face us. "I have one last suggestion."

"You're not a part of this anymore," warned Mr. Fogelman.

"Old Shep shouldn't die," he announced. "Think about it." And he was gone.

*. . . Remember all that stuff I said before*
*about having a good time? Well, forget it.*
*Things are even more messed up than before.*
*Did you ever wish you'd picked a different job*
*besides actress? . . .*

Wallace ate his lunch in total isolation in spite of the fact that the cafeteria was packed. I almost dropped my tray when I saw him, a single dot in the center of the room, no one within twenty feet of him. He was being ignored by football players and drama club members alike, not to mention everybody who got their news from the Bedford Middle School *Weekly Standard*. Wallace Wallace, hero and superstar, was now a leper.

I carried my tray in a half circle around no-man's-land, and plunked myself down across from Trudi.

"Hi," I said into the silence.

"Rachel, I'm so sorry!" Trudi blurted. "You were right all along!"

"I don't know," I mused. "Do you think there could be another explanation for how that football jersey ended up on our stage?"

"That's another thing that burns me up," Trudi muttered. "'I haven't seen that shirt all year!' What a lame excuse! Does he think we're idiots?"

"Unless he lost it months ago," I said thoughtfully. "I lose sweaters and things all the time. Don't you?"

Trudi slapped her tray, sending a shower of hot mustard into my milk. "Well, I'm breaking up with him!" she seethed. "We're finished!"

"Maybe he's telling the truth," I suggested.

She stared at me. "Are you crazy, Rachel? You were the only person who saw through that sleaze! *He* was the one who hated *Old Shep, My Pal*! *He* was the one who had a grudge against Mr. Fogelman, and detention, and the play! We were such saps to believe him! He was rotten then, and he's rotten now!"

> *. . . Why do I believe Wallace when nobody else does? Would you stick up for Brad Pitt if the whole of Hollywood turned against him?*
> *Maybe it was how he looked right at us when he said he didn't do it (Wallace, not Brad Pitt). Maybe it was the way he stuck up for the drama club on leaf-raking day. Or maybe I'm just plain stupid . . .*

"I'll bet Wallace Wallace joins up with the Giants again," Dylan announced at dinner that night.

"He just quit the Giants," I said peevishly.

"Yeah, but now he's kicked off the play," my brother argued. "So there's no reason for him not to be on the team."

My mother cocked an eyebrow. "I thought you hated Wallace Wallace now. Remember what you said when you and Dad were picking all your football things out of the yard?"

"Oh, I'll need that stuff back," Dylan said seriously.

My father looked up from his plate. "But I just spent an hour making room for it all in the garage!"

"Listen, Dylan." I sighed. "If Wallace goes back to the team, I will personally eat the biggest bug in your chamber of horrors."

That shut Dylan up (he knew I didn't joke about insects). After dinner, while he sulked, I went for a walk. I wandered in circles that got smaller and smaller, spiraling down to the center point—the neat little house on Poplar Street with the well-raked yard.

I rang the bell, and when Mrs. Wallace saw me, her face lit up, like she was drowning and I was here with a life raft.

"Hi, I'm Rachel," I greeted her. "I was one of the rakers last Sat—"

She pulled me inside. "Thank goodness! What

happened at school today? He hasn't left his room since he got home! Not even for dinner!"

"Well, it was kind of a . . ." How could I explain it to her?

Mrs. Wallace bailed me out by calling up the stairs, "Wally! Rachel's on her way up!" To me, she said urgently, "Talk to him. Please straighten this out, whatever it is!"

It's a stupid thing to admit, but I'd never been in a guy's room before. I guess I kind of expected it to look like Dylan's chamber of horrors, only worse (because an eighth grader had three extra years to collect horrifying, disgusting things). But Wallace's room was cleaner than mine, and there were no vampire coffins or tarantulas anywhere in sight. Even the football pennants and pictures were relegated to a corner. Wallace sat at the desk under a large poster of a young George Washington chopping down the cherry tree (weird decoration for a sports hero). If he was all broken-up over today, he didn't show it.

He said, "Your shoelace is untied."

Flustered, I blurted, "I want to believe you!"

He pointed to my feet. "Take a look."

"No, I mean about shredding the scripts!" I insisted.

"But how else could that scrimmage shirt have found its way to our stage?"

He shot me a sharp glance. "Someone must have planted it there to frame me."

"Who would do that?" I asked.

Wallace threw up his arms. "I'm not exactly Mr. Popularity these days."

"Well, when was the last time you saw the shirt?"

He shrugged. "Not since—I don't know—last season at least."

"Did you lend it to anybody?"

"I lent it to *everybody*!" he exclaimed. "These jerseys—they get passed around like chicken pox. It's a miracle if you finish out the schedule with all your own stuff. The whole world came tramping through that locker room after we won the championship. I had to wear my football pants home because somebody picked up my jeans by mistake."

"So it was someone in the locker room—" I mused.

"It has to be a Giant, but I don't know which one. If it's Cavanaugh, I'll rip his lungs out!"

"Think, Wallace!" I urged. "How can I help you if—"

Wallace stood up. "Help me?" he glowered. "*Help* me? When Laszlo pulled that shirt out of the paper, do you know why everybody blamed it on me?"

"Because it was your shirt—" I stammered.

He cut me off. "Because ever since day one you and that deer tick Spitzner have been building a case against me. 'Wallace is trying to mess up the play!' You must have said it fifty times. So when everybody saw my name on the jersey, they just plugged it right into what was already in the back of their minds. And now you want to *help* me? Listen, Rachel, you've helped enough!"

> *. . . I cried, Julia! Can you believe it? Right there in his room! I never cry! But it was true. Part of this was my fault, and I couldn't handle that. He tried to grab my hand, but I just had to get out of there. I ran away, and I haven't seen him since then. Tell me the truth. I can take it. Am I losing my mind? . . .*

Determined to set things right, I showed up at football practice the next day, waving the scrimmage shirt like a battle flag.

"Of course I've seen it before," said Feather Wrigley. "Everybody has."

"Where?" I asked excitedly.

"On Wallace," the big guy explained. "See? His name's on it."

"I can read!" I informed him. "But did you notice anybody else with it?"

Suddenly, the other Giants thundered down the practice field, and Feather went right along with them. That really burned me up! Just because he was a football player didn't mean it was okay for him to treat me like I didn't exist.

Incensed, I ran after that rude slob, planning to give him a piece of my mind. "Excuse me!" I called ahead. "Hey, I was talking to you!"

Without slowing, he turned his head. He seemed shocked to find me matching him stride for stride. "Get off the field!" he yelled.

"You conceited jock!" I panted. "I'm the president of the drama club—"

"Look out!" he shouted, pointing behind me.

I turned my head just in time to see a football screaming at me like a guided missile. Blindly, I threw my arms up to protect my face. I felt the pass thump into my hands. The force of the catch knocked me over, and I slid across the turf into the end zone, the ball clutched tightly to my heart.

There were three sharp whistle blasts, and Coach Wrigley ran onto the field, cheering. "Great catch! That's exactly how I want you to execute—" His eyes fell on me, and he stopped in his tracks.

Rick Falconi galloped down the field, dancing with excitement. "Sign that skinny kid up!" he cheered. "Who is he? Who made the grab?"

"The president of the drama club," Feather supplied.

"Aw, man!" cried Rick. "How come they get all the best players?"

I stood and brushed at the grass stains on my sweater. This wasn't how I'd planned it, but I had the attention of the entire team. "One of you had Wallace Wallace's scrimmage shirt from last year," I said. "Who was it?"

"What are you, the laundry police?" the coach asked in disbelief.

I stood my ground. "It's really important. Wallace is in trouble."

From the chorus of disgusted snorts, I got the idea that Wallace was about as popular with this crowd as he was with the cast and crew of *Old Shep, My Pal.*

"You're that chick from the paper!" Rick accused me. "Wallace's girlfriend!"

"You're thinking of Trudi Davis," I defended myself. "And she's not his girlfriend either."

The coach sighed. "Wallace is a big boy. He can look after himself. Now get out of my practice." He added, "Unless you want to put in some quick weight training, and we can start you at wide receiver on Saturday."

"I've got the play that night," I replied. But I guess it wasn't a serious offer because everybody laughed at me.

A few of those rotten Giants were stomping Wallace's scrimmage shirt into the wet grass, but they scattered when they saw me coming. I picked up the muddy jersey, shaking off the clumps of turf.

"Nice catch back there, kid."

I wheeled. A lone player was watching me. He pulled off his helmet, and long blond hair spilled out onto his shoulder pads. It was the mop-top (Cavanaugh) from leaf-raking day.

I held up the shirt. "Do you know anything about this?"

"Why should I help Dummy Dummy?"

"Hey, lay off Wallace!" I snapped. "You're just jealous because he's a better football player than you!"

"Better?" he snorted. "He stinks."

"You're crazy!" I stormed. "Everybody knows Wallace got the touchdown that won the championship!"

"And that's all he got!" Mop-top snapped back at me. "One touchdown and fifty thousand splinters in his butt from sitting on the bench!"

(Huh?)

Mop-top raised an eyebrow. "Wait a minute. You're his *real* girlfriend, aren't you?"

I felt a red-hot flash of anger. "I don't even *like* Wallace Wallace! Next to you, he's the biggest jerk I've ever met! For all I know, he really did shred those scripts and do all that other stuff!"

He shrugged. "Why don't you ask him?"

"Ask him?" I echoed. "He'll just say no!"

Suddenly, this big football player was laughing so hard that, even through all those pads, his entire body was shaking.

I was enraged. "What's so funny?"

"You—you don't know Dummy Dummy at all, do you?" he guffawed.

"What are you talking about?"

All that long blond hair disappeared as Cavanaugh put his helmet back on. "Wallace Wallace is a million percent honest. He wouldn't tell a lie to save his own mother from bloodthirsty cannibals." He jogged back out onto the field.

I ran after him. "Hey! How do you know so much?"

He faced me once more. "Wallace Wallace was the best friend I ever had."

(Run that by me again?)

I peered in through his face guard, searching for that sarcastic sneer. But it wasn't there.

> . . . *Julia, I know you haven't got time to read my letters and I'm only writing them for myself. But just this once I wish you were a little less famous, because I really need some help here. I don't understand what I'm feeling.*
>
> Your very confused pen pal,<br>Rachel Turner

> *P.S. Wish us luck for the performance. We're going to need it!*

# Enter...
# TRUDI DAVIS

**I** **SENT PARKER SCHMIDT** six E-mails to make sure he got it right: I was not now, nor had I ever been, Wallace's girlfriend. Or even, like, somebody who could stand to be in the same room with that creep.

*Cosmo* says that the breakup of a long-term love affair is the most traumatic time in a single woman's life. I think that means bad. *Cosmo* isn't always clear about stuff like that. The point is, I was stressed out. And opening night is the worst time for it to happen, because that's extra stress.

Even Rachel was nervous, and she was the best actress in school. When she noticed I wasn't using the regular theatrical makeup, she practically inhaled the mirror on the dressing table backstage.

"What are you smearing on your eyes? The curtain goes up in two hours!"

I spread my eye shadow with my pinkie. "It's called Heavenly Heliotrope. Love it?"

"You look like a raccoon!" she growled.

"I need to call attention to my eyes," I explained, "so that even the people in the back row can see they're hazel."

Stage fright makes Rachel crabby. "They're brown," she informed me. "Dog-poop brown."

The two of us got up and peeked through the curtain. Fifteen rows of chairs stretched back from the stage, all the way to the basketball bleachers. They were empty now, but in two hours—

Rachel turned to Leticia, who was practicing her veterinarian's rap under her breath. "How many tickets did we sell?"

"All of them," she replied. "Seven hundred and fourteen."

I gulped. "Maybe I need a little more Heavenly Heliotrope."

"Don't you dare!" snapped Rachel. "You're supposed to be Tori Lamont, not a burglar with a purple mask!"

Vito was nervously spinning the wheels of his Rollerblades, which were hanging over his shoulder. "I'd feel a lot better if—"

"Don't say it!" I cut him off.

"Why not?" he demanded. "Everybody's thinking it. We have a great play, and we owe it to him."

All around me, cast members, set designers, stagehands, lighting guys—they were nodding! Some of them even *clapped*!

"Oh, puh-*lease!*" I exploded. "Am I the only one who remembers that Wallace Wallace is worse than slime? Think about the pepper bomb! The marbles! The pancake syrup! Think about 'Old Shep, Dead Mutt'! Think about what happened four days ago! He turned our scripts into confetti and walked out on us without another word!"

I was marching back to the mirror for more Heavenly Heliotrope when I heard Rachel murmur, "Not true. He *did* say something. He said, 'Old Shep shouldn't die.'"

"Big joke!" I snorted, digging a chunk of purple makeup out of my eye. "He's a regular comedian."

"I think I know what Wallace meant," Vito said, nodding. "Somewhere around third grade, every kid in every school has to read a book where the dog dies.

Don't you remember the first time you went home crying on the bus over Old Yeller or Irish Red?"

"It was Bristle Face," said Joey tragically. "He never lived to see the words *The End.* I felt like mine shaft, underwater cave, center of the earth, low."

"Wallace is right," Everton said positively. "We have the chance to save one dog. Let's take it."

I thought I was going to croak or something! "You're *considering* this?"

Rachel's gaze traveled from face to face around the stage. "You know, it never made sense that a football player could come in straight off the field and instantly see all the things that were wrong with our production. But every time we did what he said, the play got better. And every time we didn't, the play bogged down." She looked scared. "We've got one last piece of his advice. Do we follow it?"

"Sure we do!" crowed Joey. "We'll rewrite the words to 'Farewell, Old Pal.' Maybe 'Shep beat the odds' or 'Shep is okay!'"

"What about Mr. Fogelman?" asked Nathaniel. "He'll say no for sure."

"We don't even have to tell him!" Joey enthused. "The music won't be different, just the words!"

Well, what was I supposed to do—quit? Rachel was

the drama expert, not me. I just tried out for the play to meet guys. If she thought we should do this, then so did I.

A chant started from the crew. *"No more dead dogs! No more dead dogs! . . ."*

We had a show of hands.

# Enter...

# WALLACE WALLACE

**THIS HAD GONE** on long enough! I mean, last year everyone and his grandmother lined up to tell me how wonderful I was. Now the team hated me and the drama club hated me. Around school I was the double traitor who had been dumped by Trudi Davis. I was as popular as a skunk at an outdoor wedding.

There was only one way out of this mess. I had to go back to the people who were my friends before I was a hero *or* a villain. I would call up Rick and Feather and try to convince them to forgive me.

"Hi, Mrs. Falconi. Is Rick around? It's Wallace . . ." I almost dropped the phone. "He's *where?!* Are you sure? Okay, thanks anyway. Bye."

I hung up in disbelief. Why was Rick going to see *Old Shep, My Pal*? I mean, sure, the performance was a hot ticket at Bedford Middle School, what with all the hoopla over Parker's articles. But Rick was *furious* at the play. He blamed it for the Giants' terrible season.

Maybe Feather could explain it.

"Hi, Mrs. Wrigley, it's Wallace. Could I please speak to Feather? . . . *Really? Him too? . . .*"

Now Feather was a drama fan all of a sudden? I put down the phone, head spinning. Through the kitchen window, I saw a good hair day bobbing down the street. Cavanaugh was on his way to school and *Old Shep, My Pal*! It didn't make sense. None of these guys had ever sat through a play in their lives. In fact, any one of them could be the person who had attacked the production and framed me.

My heart began to pound. If somebody hated the play enough to shred scripts and vandalize sets, the performance itself would be the sweetest target of all. It was a chance to ruin *Old Shep, My Pal* in front of seven hundred people! I had to get over there and stop it!

My hand was already on the doorknob when I froze. What did I care if the play got trashed? I wasn't part of it anymore. Come to think of it, I was banned from the performance. I'd get in trouble if Fogelman caught me anywhere near *Old Shep, My Pal*.

I thought about the dozens of hours working shoulder to shoulder in the gym; the entire cast and crew raking leaves in my yard; people like Laszlo and Rory and the Dead Mangoes, who weren't even drama nerds but who had dedicated themselves heart and soul to the play. They had written me off, but I refused to do the same to them. Maybe no one else in this town understood loyalty, but I did.

I was going to crash a play.

The parking lot looked like the freeway at rush hour, and cars lined the street in both directions. There was no chance of sneaking in the gym entrance; I was bound to be recognized in that mob scene. Luckily, the custodian's door was unlocked, and I was able to slip inside, snake my way through the connected storerooms, and let myself into the school hall.

Wouldn't you know it. Who should be standing not five feet from the door but Rachel Turner?

"Wallace, are you crazy?" she hissed. "You're not allowed to be here! What if Mr. Fogelman sees you?"

"Shhh!" I put a finger to my lips. "I think there's going to be an attack on the play tonight."

She was horrified. "How do you know?"

"A lot of the Giants are here," I said. "They're not exactly the world's biggest drama fans."

"We have to warn Mr. Fogelman!" she exclaimed.

"No!" I ordered firmly. "And don't tell the others either. They'll panic and ruin everything. Just keep your eyes open. I'll try to find a good lookout spot."

She seemed a little uncertain, but I think she trusted me. She ran off, and I slipped into Coach Wrigley's office, which also opened into the gym.

I cracked the door about an inch and peered out. The place was jam-packed—students, brothers and sisters, parents, members of the community, and even some high school kids who were Dead Mangoes fans. It seemed like the whole world was there—from the stone-faced Giants to the smiling Dr. Chechik. From little fifth graders like Dylan Turner to the president of the school board.

I tried to memorize the location of my former teammates so I could keep an eye on them during the performance. I spotted Cavanaugh a few seats down from Dylan, but the lights were already dimming before I found Rick and Feather way back in the ninth row of bleachers.

Mr. Fogelman and the Dead Mangoes took their

places on the small band platform to the right of the stage. Joey screamed, "One, two, three, *four*!" and the group exploded into their opening number.

It was louder than anybody expected—and better. From my hiding place, it looked like half the kids in the audience were waving their hands in the air, grooving with the music. For a moment, you could almost forget that this was a school play, not a rock-and-roll show. Then the curtain slowly rose on scene one of *Old Shep, My Pal*.

There were oohs and aahs from the crowd as they watched the Rollerbladers and the moving dog. Naturally, they were focused on Rory, who was even more spectacular than usual with his dogcatcher's net. But I knew the guy to keep an eye on was Spitzner. The spider-mite had never survived a single rehearsal without a couple of humongous wipeouts. I realized in surprise that I was actually rooting for him to make it. Oh, sure, he was a loudmouth and a crybaby and all that. But you had to admire the way he was risking his life on Rollerblades when he had the athletic ability of belly-button lint.

The roar of the moped shook the gym like a volcanic eruption. There were screams from the bleachers as Laszlo shot onstage and ran over Old Shep. It was a hundred times more amazing than I remembered it. The stuffed dog went flying, Nathaniel stayed on his feet, Laszlo rode into the wings, and Rory scooped up the remote-control car with his net. Clockwork precision. Awesome.

The audience leaped to its feet in a standing ovation. Mr. Fogelman brought the Dead Mangoes to a crashing finish, and Vito skated over to the fallen Old Shep, and bellowed the very first line of the play: "Check it out!"

What a feeling! Every time one of the Lamonts spoke a piece of my dialogue, it was like scoring that touchdown all over again. When I heard the audience cheering, the excitement took hold of me in my gut. I used to roll my eyes when Rachel talked about the exhilaration of opening night, but now I understood 100 percent!

She was good, too. It drove me nuts when Rachel put on that "Little Miss Actress" attitude, but tonight she was showing that she was more than just a great-looking girl. Come to think of it, everybody was *on*. The Dead Mangoes were *kicking*! Fogelman's hands were just a blur as he pounded his keyboard. The Old Shep dancers were a hit, too. When they came out to back up the Lamont kids for the first big number—"Puppy Chow Blues"—the audience clapped and stomped along with the beat of the music. There were a few anxious moments when a triumphant Vito slapped Spitzner on the back, which sent him rolling slowly forward toward the edge of the stage. But a split second before he went over, one of the dancers managed to grab him by the shirt. She whipped him around, and sent him careening into the wings. Luckily, the Void's thunderous drum solo covered up most of the crash.

None of the Giants had left their seats yet. I kept a special eye on Kevin Wilkerson, who was shifting around in his chair. He could be waiting for his chance to make a move. Rick was fidgety as well. But some of the guys were actually getting into the play—applauding and cheering with the rest of the audience. Amazingly, Cavanaugh seemed to be one of them, but that was probably an act. My ex–best friend could be Mr. Happy while plotting the end of the world. Now *there* was a guy who belonged in drama. His whole life was an award-winning performance.

I was so wrapped up in the guys and the play, that I almost missed the click behind me. I spun around. There, by the opposite door stood Coach Wrigley. The jig was up.

I smiled weakly. "Great play, huh, Coach?"

He glared at me. "You're not supposed to be here, Wallace."

"Don't kick me out," I pleaded. "You can put me back on detention starting Monday, but I really need to see this."

"Ever heard of school rules?"

I admit it. I was sweating. "I can explain—"

I fell silent while he looked me over. Finally, he said, "I don't want an explanation, I want some of that famous honesty. Should I be worried about what you're doing here tonight?"

"It's cool, Coach. You can trust me."

"I hope so," he growled. "Or your next appearance at practice will be as the tackling dummy." And with that he left me to my spying.

Good old Coach Wrigley! I hurried back to my post at the door to check on the suspects. It was a madhouse out there. The Dead Mangoes had swung into their second big song, "Shep's the Man (Even Though He's a Dog)," and the entire audience was dancing. Onstage, the Lamont family was singing, the thunderstorm was raging, and the Old Shep dancers were riling the crowd. A lot of the kids were actually standing on their chairs, punching the air in time to the heavy beat. Anxiously, I searched the riot for the Giants. There was Cavanaugh; Kevin; Feather, and right beside him—my breath caught in my throat. Rick's seat was empty.

In desperation, I scoured the dancing, seething mass of humanity that covered the bleachers. The quarterback was nowhere to be found. I was just beginning to feel cold panic when I spotted him. He had made his way to the end of the row, and was climbing down the side of the bleachers. He dropped to the gym floor, unnoticed by the partying crowd.

I ran to the other door and opened it a crack. Rick slipped out of the auditorium and headed down the hall. I waited for him to turn right, then ran to the corner. There was a banging sound and muted curses.

I peered around the corner, and smiled in spite of myself. A couple of times every year, Rick always forgot his locker combination. Usually, the custodian had to come to cut off the lock with a hacksaw.

"Aw, great! Why tonight?" he muttered, twisting and yanking. By sheer luck, he hit upon the right number, and the lock came off. He threw open the vented door and rummaged through his stuff, coming up with a small rectangular object.

I squinted. What was that thing? Images flashed

through my mind like somebody was channel-surfing with a remote hooked up to my brain. I pictured our cast, holding their noses and running from a stink bomb on the stage. Or jumping around and scratching because a container of itching powder had been dumped into the vent and blown over everybody. The vision changed. Now the actors were bumping into each other in the darkness. That box was some kind of electric gizmo that shorted out the lights.

Rick shut his locker and headed back toward me. I still couldn't identify what was in his hand, but it was now or never. If I let him pass, he'd be three steps from the stage door. I had to stop him.

When he rounded the corner, I pounced, jerking whatever it was out of his hand. Without even looking at it, I hurled it with all my might down the hall.

Rick gawked in amazement and then outrage. "Are you crazy, Wallace?"

"You've got nothing to say, Rick!" I seethed. "I know you're upset about me and the Giants, but that doesn't give you the right to declare war on the play! You busted up rehearsals, terrorized the cast—"

"Wait a minute!" he cried in shock. "You think all that was *me*?!"

Angrily, I pointed down the hall. "Then what

were you doing with that—that—*thing*?"

Rick grabbed me by the shirt and hauled me over to where the mysterious object lay broken on the terrazzo floor. It was a small Kodak box camera, the kind you throw out after one roll of film.

I looked at him in confusion. "A camera?"

He glowered at me. "I was *going* to take a couple of pictures for my good friend Wallace who wasn't allowed to be here tonight. I thought maybe it would help patch things up between us if I gave them to you as a present, since you're *persona nongratitude* at the play."

"But—you hate me!" I managed.

"I hate what you *did*, not you!" he stormed. "You jerk! How could you think I'd be rotten enough to do all that stuff to the play?"

I shrugged apologetically. "I knew it had to be a Giant—"

"How come?"

"You're the ones with a gripe against *Old Shep, My Pal*," I explained. "Plus, I got framed with an old scrimmage shirt. Who else could have had one besides a Giant?"

"Millions of people," Rick argued. "After the championship last year, anything with your name on it was an instant souvenir. All those screaming kids—they cleaned you out!"

"Wait a minute!" I said excitedly. "That celebration in the locker room—Coach Wrigley has the whole thing on videotape!"

Joey Quick's mournful guitar solo wailed in through the crack in the door as we riffled through the boxes of VHS cassettes in Coach Wrigley's office.

"Hey," Rick commented, pulling another carton from under the desk. "What happened to all that great music? It's getting, you know, depressing."

I looked at my watch. "It's supposed to. We're getting near the end of the play. Old Shep dies pretty soon."

"Old Shep *dies*?" He looked shocked. "What's the point of having a whole story about a dog if he's only going to die?"

I rolled my eyes. "If someone had said that to Zack Paris fifty years ago, we both wouldn't be here right now. Jackpot," I added, pulling out a tape marked Postgame Celeb. Nov. '99.

I popped the cassette into the VCR and hit *play*. Last year's celebration appeared on the monitor, trembled and stabilized.

The video brought it all back to me—a crazy, happy afternoon. I was already soaked with Gatorade by the time my teammates carried me into the locker room. Players were shaking bottles of soda and spraying them in all directions. Then came the parents, puffed up with pride, and finally the kids, our nutty fans, out of their minds with happiness. We had the volume off, but my memory provided the sound—a never-ending shriek of joy, punctuated by chants of "Way to go!" and "Number one!"

I could see Rick's face growing long and tragic as he stared glumly at the screen. I put an arm around his shoulders. "Come on, Rick. It was a football game, not world peace."

He grimaced. "It was world peace to me! But you don't even care!"

"That's not true. I wouldn't trade it for anything. But it's *over*! We can't live in the past."

He sighed. "Yeah, I know. It just kills me that I'll never again get to see the—the gloriosity of you sailing through the air to save the nick of time."

I slapped him on the back. "Don't worry, Rick. You'll see plenty of gloriosity in your life."

Suddenly, Rick pointed at the screen. "Stop the tape!"

I dove at the VCR and hit *pause*. We both knelt in front of the TV. In the frozen flickering picture, Feather held the championship trophy over his head. Below his elbow, in the background, was my open locker. A small hand was reaching inside and pulling out—yes!—my scrimmage shirt.

"Who is it?" asked Rick.

It was impossible to see because Kevin had just launched an entire barrel of Gatorade at Feather. The mass of orange liquid exploded out of the bucket and was captured on our screen—completely blocking the thief's face.

"Watch carefully," I ordered, and pushed *play*.

*Sploosh!* The Gatorade hit Feather full in the chest, and the party raged on.

I stared at the TV. "Can you see him?"

Rick shook his head. "Too many people in the way."

Determinedly, I backed up the tape. This time, I played it in super slo-mo. Now the Gatorade bomb seemed to crawl out of the bucket. We concentrated hard as it floated toward Feather like a balloon.

"There's the hand!" exclaimed Rick.

But the culprit's face was still blocked by the big glob of orange. He pulled my jersey out of the locker, and turned to rejoin the celebration where he'd disappear into the mob.

"Show your face!" I breathed at the hidden bandit.

At that moment, the Gatorade reached Feather. In slow motion, the big mass turned to millions of tiny droplets shooting out in all directions.

"There he is!" cried Rick.

I punched *pause*. Through the freeze-frame orange spray, I could just make out the face of the thief, the guy who set me up, the enemy of the play.

Oh, boy.

The stage entrance was locked for the performance. With a sense of deep purpose, I pounded and kicked at it until Laszlo swung the door wide.

He clapped me on both shoulders and shook my hand. "Wallace! You came!" Then he saw Rick, and his grin disappeared. "Hold it—"

I stepped in the door before he could slam it on us. "Don't let anybody else backstage!" I ordered.

"But, Wallace—"

Rick and I ran off into the wings, leaving Laszlo gaping after us.

Rick stumbled and went down. I dropped to my knees to see what had tripped him up. It was the basket that was home to the injured Old Shep. I gazed out onto the stage. Leticia, the veterinarian, had just begun her rap.

I frowned. The dog was supposed to be dead—in the basket—onstage. What was the basket doing here? Where was Old Shep? More important, where was *he*?

Desperately, I spun all around. There were millions of great hiding places. Curtains, equipment, and scenery provided countless nooks, crannies, and alcoves.

"It's too dark," Rick complained. "If he's here, we'll never find him."

And as he got to his feet, a high-pitched voice cried, "Ow!"

I gawked. Underneath Rick's sneaker was another sneaker, protruding from behind a small curtain. Rick reached around and hauled out the culprit.

Dylan Turner.

"Dylan, are you crazy?" I rasped.

"Me, crazy?" he shot right back. "I'm not the one who killed the Giants!" He shook his arm free and glared at Rick. "And I'll bet you were in on it! You stank all season on purpose!"

"No way!" Rick defended himself. "I stank naturally!"

I tried reason. "Look, Dylan, this is *wrong*! All these guys, the actors and crew—they've put so much work into this play! How can you wreck it for them? For your own sister?"

He looked at me in scorn. "The Giants work hard, too, you know."

"Then punish *me*! *I'm* the traitor!" I spread my arms wide. "Here, take a shot. A punch, a kick—whatever you want. Just leave the play alone."

"And get beaten up?" he sneered. "I don't think so."

"We won't lay a finger on you," Rick promised. "Just tell us what you did."

A wicked smile took hold of Dylan's features. "It's too late to stop it."

"Stop what?" I demanded.

His grin became wild. "I put a cherry bomb on Old Shep."

"*Where's* Old Shep?" I exclaimed. "He's supposed to be dead!"

"They changed the ending!" he told us. "They said it was—" he started to giggle—"*your* idea!"

My attention snapped back to the stage. Leticia was finishing off her big number. But instead of delivering the bad news, she rapped:

"This is no hype, this is no jive,
Your dog, Old Shep, is still alive!"

And suddenly, there he was, the world's most famous dead dog, not dead at all. Back on his remote-control car, Old Shep passed through the dog door of the Lamont house into the beam of a single spotlight. I felt like I was watching someone coming back from the afterlife.

The audience went crazy. Even the kids who didn't know the story of *Old Shep, My Pal* had for sure read *Sounder* or *Old Yeller*, and were bracing themselves for the tragic conclusion. Instead, our Old Shep returned like a sunrise, moving across the stage bathed in pink light. If Zack Paris himself could have heard the roar in our gym that night, he would have gone back in time and changed his own ending. It might have cost him the Gunhold Award, but he would have had a better book, and a whole lot more satisfied readers.

I was mesmerized. I couldn't take my eyes off Old Shep as he closed in on the Lamont kids. He was magical, supernatural—all at once, I spotted the red of the cherry bomb stuck in the crook of his paw—*he was dynamite on wheels!*

I snatched the pillow from Old Shep's basket and ran out onstage.

"Wallace?!" It came from all directions and a lot of different throats. I recognized Rachel and Coach Wrigley and Mr. Fogelman in there somewhere, but I had no time to think about that now.

The glowing dot of orange on the cherry bomb's wick was burned all the way down. I wasn't going to make it.

I hurled myself at the stuffed dog in a flying desperation leap. As my feet left the floor, I was aware of a split second of complete silence—not a sound from the audience, the band, or the cast. I was in the air, and Old Shep was getting closer, and I held the pillow over my face, and—

*BOOM!!!*

Old Shep exploded just as I landed on top of him. I felt the blast through the cushion. Instantly, I was engulfed in a whirlwind of flying plush animal hair and pillow stuffing. I gasped for breath and inhaled a throatful of smoke and fluff.

"*Wallace!*" Rachel threw herself on top of me and pulled me from Old Shep. I bounced off her, she somersaulted over me, and we tumbled along the stage. Finally we rolled to a halt at the feet of the other cast members. Trudi, Vito, and Nathaniel gawked down at us, mute with shock.

The audience was cowed, and I didn't blame them. Picture it: Rachel and I were covered with gray soot and charred brown fur. A plume of thick smoke rose from the now-naked stuffed dog, which smoldered amid piles of its own hair. The wheels of the remote control car were spinning, but I had busted the toy with my crash landing. It wasn't going anywhere. Neither was Old Shep.

From the gym floor and bleachers, over fourteen hundred wide eyes stared up at us. Dr. Chechik and some of the teachers were halted halfway to the stage. I guess they stopped because they weren't really sure if all this was an accident or just a very weird part of the show.

The cast looked to Mr. Fogelman, but our director stood frozen like a block of ice, white to the ears before his keyboard.

That was when Rachel showed why she was the president of the drama club. In the middle of all that chaos, she struggled to her feet, elbowed Trudi in the ribs, and whispered, "The show must go on!"

The Lamonts stared at her.

"What?" Trudi hissed.

"The show *must* go on!"

And with that, she nodded to the band. Joey Quick played the opening chords of "Farewell, Old Pal," and the Dead Mangoes, even Mr. Fogelman, joined in.

I was trying to slither behind the scenery board of the Lamont house. But as soon as the singing began, I sat up in surprise. It wasn't "Farewell, old pal!" that the Lamont kids were belting out at top volume; instead they chorused:

"Shep is okay! Hip hip hooray!
He'll live to bark another day!"

Of course! They had to change the words to fit the new ending!

The problem was that Shep *wasn't* okay. Shep was on fire. Shep was belching smoke at seven hundred astounded spectators.

All at once, waves of laughter and applause filled the gym. The audience was on its feet again, roaring its approval of this hilarious ending. The four bewildered Lamonts could only sing on:

"Shep is okay! His health is super!
He's strong as the shaft of his pooper scooper!"

At that moment, the fire spread from Old Shep down into the car. With a loud pop, the remote-control toy short-circuited and blew. The crowd howled with mirth as flames shot up six inches from the stuffed dog. Still on my knees, I crawled back out onto the stage and tried to blow out the fire, but it was no use. I had to beat down the blaze with what was left of the pillow from Old Shep's basket.

A final puff of smoke dispersed just as the song and the play came to a close. The roar of the crowd was deafening, but I missed most of it. Rachel yanked me up by the collar and frog-marched me into the wings.

"He took off, Wallace!" Rick called to me. "I turned my back for a second and—"

"Aha!" Rachel thrust her index finger half an inch from Rick's eye. She turned to me. "Was it him, Wallace? Is this the low-down scum who *ruined* our play?"

"Ruined?" repeated Trudi in disbelief. "We're a smash! Listen!" She pointed onstage where the tremendous ovation raged on. Vito and Nathaniel beckoned, and the rest of the cast was straggling out to accept the adulation of an enraptured audience.

"Bravo!"

"Best play I ever saw!"

"Old Shep rocks!"

"They're laughing at us!" Rachel shrieked. "And why not? We nursed a dog back to health only to have him blow up like a hand grenade! Who was it, Wallace? Who did this to us?"

Oh, how my heart went out to Rachel just then. Her precious play had literally exploded; her acting career, her life's dream, had been converted into a big joke; she was humiliated in front of her parents, her classmates, and half the town; and now she was about to learn that her own little brother was the cause of it all.

Poor Rachel, who believed me when nobody else would—who even risked her life to save me from a burning stuffed animal! I had to find a way to make this easy on her. But how?

"It was me," I blurted.

Rick gasped. *"What?"*

I cut him off with a razor-sharp look. "It's been me all along," I went on. "I'm sorry."

She hauled off and punched me in the stomach. I barely felt the pain through my horror and disbelief at what I had done.

After fourteen years of total honesty, I, Wallace Wallace, had told a lie!

# Enter...

# RACHEL TURNER

*Dear Julia,*
    *So much has happened! Where do I start?*
*Let's just say that the next time you run into*
*Brad Pitt around Hollywood, you owe him a*
*big apology . . .*

My parents grounded Dylan for eight hundred years. He almost got away with it. After the play, he ran straight home and hid in a tree. When we finally found him (just before midnight), he was already blubbering lame excuses. If he'd kept his mouth shut, he might even have pulled it off.

I tried to forgive him. Well, not really. But he *was*

my brother (and would be in the next room for at least eight hundred years), so I was stuck with him. I swallowed my anger and visited him on day one of his sentence. I even brought a little gift, a (repulsive) plastic skull with nasty protruding eyeballs.

"Thanks, Rach. I love it! But—" Dylan looked embarrassed "—don't you hate me?" He studied the carpet. "Sorry about yesterday. And, you know, all those other times."

"Well, I figured the chamber of horrors could use a little brightening up," I told him. "Especially since you're going to be spending a lot of time here for the next eight hundred years."

Dylan shrugged. "Mom was just mad. I'll bet I'm out in half that."

I laughed. "Hey, Dylan, do you have any idea why Wallace tried to take the rap for you?"

"Sure." He brightened. "Because he's the greatest!"

"The greatest?" I echoed. "Last night you detonated the whole world just because you were mad at him!"

"But he proved one thing," Dylan enthused. "He's still got the moves!" He swiveled his computer monitor to face me. He was logged onto porkzit.com, where Parker posted all the articles he wrote for the *Standard*.

Right on page one was a picture of Wallace leaping

onto the exploding Old Shep. I blinked in surprise. It was exactly the same photograph as the big touchdown last year, with the stuffed dog taking the place of the football.

## Parker Schmidt's E-News Page
# TOUCHDOWN STAGE LEFT!
by Parker Schmidt, Staff Reporter

The truth has finally come out. Wallace Wallace faked his own expulsion from *Old Shep, My Pal* only to set up the surprise of the century for his shock appearance in an amazing comedy ending—a hilarious canine replay of last year's championship touchdown. If this doesn't erase the incomplete from his English grade, nothing will.

Now it's time for Rachel Turner to step down and allow this brilliant athlete-actor-director to assume the presidency of the drama club.

Wallace could not be reached for comment, but according to on-again/off-again girlfriend Trudi Davis . . .

I shook my head. "If he picked up a paintbrush, they'd call him Picasso."

"Is it true that he and Trudi got back together?" asked Dylan. "And he's taking over your job in the drama club?"

"Porker Zit is delusional. He gets his facts in fantasy-land."

Dylan pointed over to his desk. "Hey, Rach. I've got a letter of yours. It must have come yesterday. It was stuck to my package from the Ooze of the Month Club."

I picked up the envelope by the edges and brushed it off on his pillow. "Dylan," I said, annoyed, "I like to get my mail the day it arrives. And that little green spot better not be ooze."

Suddenly, my eyes fell on the postmark—*Hollywood, CA*. There was no return address, just the scrawled initials *JR*.

I didn't believe it. I still didn't believe it when I had the short note open right in front of me:

> *Dear Rachel,*
>    *I've starred in enough romantic comedies to know one when I see it. Take my word for it—you are crazy about this guy Wallace. Don't let him get away.*
>
>                *Yours truly,*
>                *Julia Roberts*

Two questions jolted through my body like four thousand volts of electricity: 1) Why didn't I know that? And 2) Why didn't I know it *YESTERDAY*?!!

Wallace was ignoring me at school on Monday. Not that Julia's predictions had any chance of coming true after I'd punched him, but at least I wanted to say I was sorry. I guess he was pretty mad at me, and I couldn't really blame him. For over a month, I'd treated him like a criminal. And not only was he innocent, but the true culprit turned out to be my own flesh and blood.

I finally cornered him with a move so immature it was worthy of Trudi. In the cafeteria line, I saw Wallace filling up a taco. I picked up the salsa bowl and dumped out the entire thing onto my plate. When he reached the empty container, I came up behind him.

"Here, take some of mine," I offered. "I got a little carried away."

"That's okay," he mumbled, and turned his back on me. He sure didn't sound like the Wallace *I* knew (who would stick out that iron jaw and tell the king of the world what he thought of him). It made me really sad to think that Wallace would rather choke down a dry taco than be forced to look at me.

I followed him to an open table. "I have to talk to you."

"No." He pushed away his taco. "*I* have to talk to *you*. Listen, Rachel. I lied."

"I know," I said soothingly. "Dylan's serving hard time in his Chamber of Horrors."

He shook his head. "You don't understand. I never lie. It just doesn't happen—"

"It's okay," I interrupted.

"I don't know what came over me. I mean, what was I thinking? I guess—well, Old Shep blew up, and you were so upset—"

I scooped up a spoonful of salsa from my mountain and dumped it on his taco. "It was sweet," I told him. "Really sweet."

His response to that was to eat his lunch. (Oh, Julia, why couldn't your letter have come just a little bit sooner? Why couldn't my rotten brother have given it to me when it arrived? Thanks to the Ooze of the Month Club, I had chased this guy away forever!)

Then he said, "Now that the play's over, maybe we could get together sometime. You know, if you want."

I always figured that the first time a guy asked me out, the words would resound like thunderclaps, deep and romantic (or at least *different*). But no, it was

Wallace's usual voice, his here's-the-truth, take-it-or-leave-it style.

Did I want to get together with Wallace? Was Julia Roberts an actress? (Definitely.)

And then it hit me.

"There's a problem," I admitted. "What about Trudi? We've been friends since third grade. And, well, you've probably noticed that she totally loves you. You and me hanging out—do you think she could handle it?"

At that moment, Trudi marched into the cafeteria with that mop-topped friend of Wallace's, Steve Cavanaugh.

"Hey, Rachel!" Dragging Steve behind her, she rushed over and sat down at our table, depositing him on the bench beside her.

"Nice lunch," the big football player remarked to me. "I see you've got the salsa food group pretty much covered."

Trudi guffawed like a braying donkey. I'd heard that (un)magical sound before. Trudi didn't laugh with her mouth; she laughed with her hormones. My friend had locked her homing mechanism on another guy.

Wallace had a piece of advice for his former

teammate. "If you see her talking to Parker, leave town."

Steve eased himself a little farther down the bench from where Trudi was plastered up against him. "I hear Hong Kong is nice this time of year."

"Isn't he hot?" Trudi whispered to me. "And we have *so* much in common! I would *kill* for his hair!" She ruffled the blond mop-top. "Hey, I'm going to rent *Demolition Ninja Bombers* to watch after school. Who wants to come?"

All at once, Wallace and I were grinning at each other. (Julia Roberts, you're a wise woman.)

"We're in," I agreed.

The mop-top looked uncertain.

Wallace sighed. "Come on, Steve. It's just like *Old Shep, My Pal*. Everything blows up at the end."

Steve clasped his hands together in mock joy. "Oh, Doofus Doofus, really? Wally and Stevie, together again! It'll be just like the good old days. Plus I hear you're coming back to the Giants on Saturday. We've kept your spot on the bench all nice and warm for you."

Wallace just smiled (I said it before; nice teeth for a football player).

"I'll take that spot any day of the week," he replied. "It's exactly where I want to be."

I know the truth when I hear it.

# LOOKING FOR MORE FROM GORDON KORMAN?

Turn the page to start reading!

# chapter 1

# THE NICKNAMERS

THE SUBSTITUTE TEACHER must have been six-feet-five, and solid as an oak tree. He shrugged his massive shoulders out of his warm-up jacket, revealing a barrel chest and giant muscles rippling under his T-shirt.

In the back row, Wiley Adamson opened his notebook to a clean page, and wrote: *King Kong?*

At the next desk, Jeff Greenbaum examined the paper critically. His brown eyes narrowed, as they always did when he was deep in thought. Deliberately, he reached out his pencil and drew a line through the nickname. Below it, he printed: *The Incredible Hulk?*

Wiley flashed a grudging grin of admiration, but

he crossed that one out too, and added: *Tiny?*

This brought a snicker from Jeff, which he swallowed when the new teacher began to speak.

"I guess I don't look very much like Mrs. Regan." He chuckled in a deep voice. This was true. The regular teacher stood four-feet-nine, and was wispy and white-haired. She had just retired to Florida. "I'll be taking over this class until a permanent replacement is found."

An uncomfortable murmur passed through the room. It wasn't so bad losing Mrs. Regan, and having a sub was usually a license to goof off. But this sub was obviously no pushover. He looked like the Terminator.

Through the speech, Wiley and Jeff continued to trade ideas.

*Hercules?*
*Mr. E. Normous?*

But nothing seemed just right. And if there was anything the two nicknamers of 6B knew for certain, it was that a true nickname had to fit perfectly.

"Now, some of you might recognize me as the assistant coach of the football team over at the high school," the big teacher was saying. "I never expected to wind up in sixth grade but, you know, with budget cuts—"

*Musclehead?*
*Conan the Grammarian?*

He picked up the chalk and wrote his name on the board. "I'm Mr. Hughes."

Wiley and Jeff exchanged a look of pure delight.

Peter Widman was the leadoff hitter in the softball game at recess. He already had a nickname, courtesy of Wiley and Jeff. Because of the thin blond streak in his jet-black hair, he was known affectionately as Skunk. He tapped his bat on home plate and assumed his stance.

"Hey, Skunk," said Wiley from his catcher's crouch. "What do you think of Mr. Huge?"

Peter stared at him for a moment, then threw back his head and laughed. "Mr. Huge!" he cackled. "I get it. That's funny!"

"What's the holdup?" called Jeff from the pitcher's mound.

"We're talking about Mr. Huge!" roared Peter.

Jeff pretended not to understand. "You mean Mr.

Hughes?" he yelled back with a wink aimed at Wiley.

"No, Mr. *Huge!*"

Peter got a hit. Soon he and the first baseman were laughing over the new nickname. When Peter stole second and then third, the entire infield was brought in on the joke. By the end of the inning, the word was out. Raymond Vaughn, the shortstop, had even taught himself how to burp "Mr. Huge" at top volume. Most of what Raymond said was communicated by a series of belches. This talent had earned him the nickname Gasbag.

"Mr. Huge" spread through the softball game like a case of measles. Every few seconds a burst of laughter or shout of approval sprang up as the new nickname was passed from mouth to mouth.

"Mr.—Oh, I get it! Because he's so big!"

"And his name—Hughes, Huge—"

"Why didn't *I* think of that?"

Wiley looked at his watch. "Eleven minutes and forty-five seconds."

"That's got to be our fastest time ever," Jeff said proudly.

Then the bush in front of them sneezed. Charles Rossi sprang up out of the scratchy branches.

"I'm onto you guys!" he raged. "Don't think I can't

see what you're up to. You just got everybody to call the new teacher Mr. Huge."

Wiley shrugged. "The guy's enormous and his name is Hughes. It was only a matter of time before somebody came up with it."

"But you did. You do it all the time," Charles accused them. "I'll bet it's like a game to you jerks."

Wiley snorted in disgust. "Ignore him," he advised Jeff. "You know what this is about, and it has nothing to do with Mr. Huge. Charles just doesn't like being called Snoopy."

Charles Rossi's face turned beet red. If looks could kill, Wiley and Jeff would have fallen down dead right on the spot. "Snoopy is a stupid nickname! A mean nickname! A *dog's* nickname!"

"Face it," Jeff said reasonably. "You know why everyone calls you Snoopy? Because you spend more time minding other people's business than your own."

Wiley nodded in agreement. "Where did we find you just now? In the bushes, snooping."

"I was not!" Charles raged. "I was tying my shoe. *You're* the ones who thought up Snoopy. And you blabbed it all over the world. Exactly like you just did with Mr. Huge!"

Jeff rolled his eyes. "If Snoopy was a bad nickname

nobody else would even bother repeating it. You're Snoopy because you're the biggest snoop in school. It's a well-known fact that a nickname will never stick if it's not the right one."

"Baloney!" Charles accused. "You can make any name stick if you say it often enough."

"No way," said Jeff.

"We'll prove it," Wiley added. "Pick a kid—any kid— and we'll give him a nickname that's totally, completely, absolutely wrong. You'll see. It won't stick."

Charles's eyes narrowed. "What's in it for me if *I'm* right?"

Wiley shrugged. "What have you got in mind?"

"I want a new nickname," Charles said instantly. "A good nickname. A *person's* nickname."

"It's a deal," agreed Jeff. With a sweep of his arm, he indicated the playground. "All we need now is a guinea pig for our experiment."

The three looked around. Most of the softball players already had nicknames. Kelly Warnover was known as Warmed-Over-Leftovers; Christy Jones was Crusty Bones; Gordon Wu's monster appetite had earned him the title Smorgas-Gord; identical twin brothers Dinky and Stan were dubbed Stinky and Dan; and of course, Gasbag and Skunk.

"I've got it," said Charles. "Him."

Wiley and Jeff followed the direction of his pointing finger. There stood Mike Smith, a tall blond boy from 6A. Mike was in the midst of a spirited game of dodgeball, but he definitely wasn't participating. He wasn't even watching. Actually, he wasn't doing anything.

Wiley and Jeff groaned in unison. They knew it wasn't going to be easy to come up with a nickname, good *or* bad, for Mike Smith. Mike was simply the blandest student in the history of Old Orchard Public School (called OOPS, thanks to the two nicknamers). He was neither happy nor unhappy. He didn't really have any friends, but no one was his enemy. What was he like? What was his favorite food? Did he watch TV? Was he a sports fan? Computer nerd? Musician? *Martian?* Nobody really knew.

"Come on, Snoopy," Wiley wheedled. "Pick somebody else. That guy's so *nothing!* If we can't figure out what he *is*, how can we nickname him what he *isn't?*"

Charles folded his arms in front of him. "He's my choice."

Jeff threw his hands in the air. "What are you supposed to call a blob like that—Iceman?"

"That's it!" crowed Wiley. "Iceman!" He turned to

Charles. "If that name sticks, I'll eat your backpack!"

The bell rang to signal the end of recess. Wiley, Jeff, and Charles joined the parade to the door.

Charles elbowed Jeff in the ribs. "I don't hear anything."

Jeff frowned. "What are you listening for—bird calls?"

Charles gestured toward Mike Smith. "You have to call him Iceman. You know, spread it around. Just like you did with Mr. Huge."

Jeff looked helpless. "I feel so stupid. He's about as cool as a loaf of bread. Why don't *you* do it, Snoopy?"

"It only works when it's you."

"Oh, all right," sighed Wiley. He waved at Mike and piped up, "Hey, Iceman!"

The tall boy from 6A didn't even look up. They were obviously talking to somebody else.

Wiley nudged Jeff. "This is one bet we can't lose."